MILTON MUST coat

THE THREE BEASTS
& THE UNICORNS

Sally E K Warner

For my children

Torsten, Sarocha & Ione

ACKNOWLEDGMENTS

Thank you to my children for their inspiration and encouragement. To my daughters, for dressing up in costume and acting, as we trailed the countryside looking for film locations. To my sister, for walking coastlines looking for ancient Mesolithic sites and standing stones. To my parents for leaving me purple notes. To Mark and Ben Atkinson and Candice, for letting me photograph and film their horse with a unicorn horn on. And to Vicki for testing it out on her horse. To Janet, Ruth and Carmen, for reading my first drafts. And to my old English teachers, Mr. Bailey and Mr. Seath, who encouraged me with my stories.

"Save me from the lion's mouth: for thou hast heard me from the horns of the unicorns." Psalms 22:21

LOST ANCIENT MESOLITHIC TEXT
(A possible precursor to Ogham)

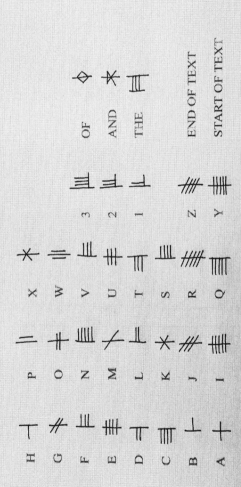

A	I	Y	START OF TEXT
B	J	Z	END OF TEXT
C	K	R	
D	L	T	1	THE
E	M	U	2	AND
F	N	V	3	OF
G	O	W		
H	P	X		
Q				
S				

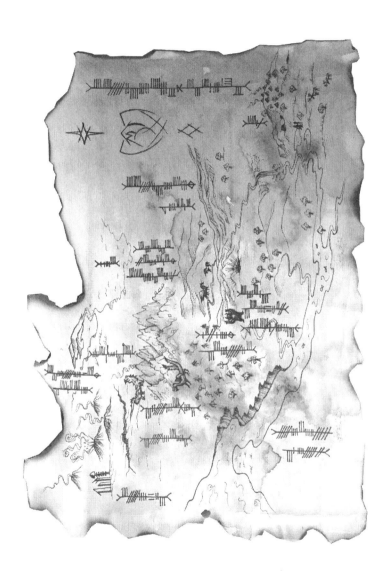

I

THE WATERFALL

*C*old, *the water was, cool and refreshing.*

Olga splashed her face in the pool at the base of the waterfall. The water poured over the cliff some ninety feet above her, a steady cascade, though much less than usual after this hot, dry weather. It was peaceful and quiet, just the gentle sound of the waterfall and birds calling in the end of a late afternoon.

Her tunic of linen tied loosely around her waist with a cord of leather, a band of leather around her arm that she'd stuck a hawk's feather in, and a leather cord necklace hung from her neck from which was bound a stone and another hawk's feather. Two small plaits framed her face while the rest of her long dark hair, left loose, reached down her back. She picked up the spear she'd been carving, that rested against the rock beside her, and set off up the bank following the worn path back to her village. A hundred strong settlement, made up of huts and a few small caves in the sandstone, lay at the hill top.

At the edge of the settlement were some cave dwellings, natural recesses carved out by the elements over time, with rooms extended by generations before them. Here, in one of them, she joined her older sister Heather and her mother making a meal of fresh fish, with deer-milk curds, leaves and tubers. This they cooked together over an open fire in the central space in their cave, the smoke channelled outside through an opening high up in the rock.

The faint hum of the daily goings on of the other tribes people drifted in. A drum beat out a tattoo, heralding the end of the day and the beginning of the balmy summer evening. A group of elders sat in a circle round a large fire pit, drinking beer and gripped in discussions. A squad of wood hens ran across the clearing and into their straw coop. Two young children laughed, running after them. And a capercaillie called in the woodlands below.

The warm summer evening faded and night fell.

II

THE MESSENGER

Heather woke up.

An eerie golden glow seeped through the wattle hazel door and into the cave. She sat up on her bed of furs and bracken and rubbed her eyes. It wasn't morning. No one else was awake.

The half finished weaving hung against the opposite wall, bundles of madder root, weld and woad hung up drying. In a carved recess in the soft sandstone, chopped herbs and roots lay on the slate slab where food was prepared, alongside eggs, crab apples, bilberries and haws in reed woven baskets. Nothing had changed.

Cautiously she crept across the rough swept floor, past her sleeping sister Olga. With a bit of effort she moved aside the hazel door that shut out the night and its creatures. Now the strange glow flooded inside. She moved down towards the entrance of the cave. There was something there, ...outside, something stirred the bracken, a soft thud, a twig cracked, a snort....

With some deliberation Heather eased her head around the edge of the rock. Standing before her, a creature broad and tall, bright and glowing, the source of the strange light. She gasped again, unable to move or take her eyes off the one long, pointed, twisted horn that grew out of its head just above its eyes. And that pointed directly at her.

It was a unicorn.

It was 5,202 BC.

An old time, an ancient time, an age that had disintegrated while written in history with the missing holes never found. Stories of men passed down, myths, part truth, unfolded.

Unicorns were feared. And never seen. They'd killed the tribespeople; at first a deer, then a dog, then a child. Or so the tales of old said.

It was said that early Stone Age Man had hunted them down for their horns and their magical properties, driven them away almost to extinction, only their faded image on cave walls remained like ghosts of past.

But Heather still froze. She should raise the alarm, shout out, yet something in the look in this beast's eyes told her not to.

"Help us," the unicorn softly breathed, in its strange melodic horse-like voice. "I am the Messenger Unicorn, I know your soul is gentle, ...will you help us?"

Heather's jaw dropped, it spoke! Logic told her to be afraid, but she felt her fears subside, this creature, this 'unicorn' had a reassuring and quite commanding aura. Relaxing a little, though all her senses still bristling with the adrenalin, like fire running through her veins, she reached out shakily and gently touched the unicorn's neck.

This unicorn was a magnificent beast. So much like a horse in stance and manner, yet much larger and glowing, not just literally with this strange light, but also with strength and power; a strong mare. Her coat was a beautiful golden colour, and her mane fell about her head and neck in long cream blonde tassels. Her horn, the fiercest part of her, grew in a spiral, a little irregular, out of her head, pale and golden like the rest of her.

This glowing light was tangible, and fell off her coat like dust when Heather touched her. She was drawn to her, she was magnetic, she was curious and intriguing. Heather could do nothing other than obey her when she whinnied, "Get on my back and I will show you why we need your help."

"You, you're incredible," said Heather, when words eventually came out of her mouth. And, as if under a spell, she stood on a rock, took a handful of mane above her withers, hauled herself up and slipped her leg across the unicorn's broad back. She sat there in her woad-blue tunic. Dark hair, long and untidy from sleep, lifted in the light breeze. The Messenger Unicorn turned briskly, pawed the ground with her left hoof, pranced a couple of steps back and with a flick of her long tail, took off at tremendous speed. Heather let out a shriek, she'd ridden horses before, but this was nothing like it.

The Messenger Unicorn was moving so fast, like an arrow shot from a yew bow, flashing through the trees away from Heather's home. Heather lost her grip and swung down to one side, hanging on for dear life with just one leg and a handful of mane. Realising the unicorn wasn't going to let up speed she summoned up her energy and with all her will, she hauled herself round and back on top, so that she gripped the unicorn's flanks with both thighs. The power and thundering hooves took her breath away.

They left the wooded hill slopes, the deer lands, and galloped past the sacred caves used by their ancestors, the Sacre Ogof, full of paintings and bones from the time before the ice. They crossed hills and jumped streams, passing the ancient Water Henge, Duer Aor; a place of healing and transformation, a passage of water carved into the landscape. Like the standing stones at Solas Aor, the Sun Temple near Heather's home, Duer Aor was set to revere the sun. Both marking the solstices and equinoxes that shaped their seasons. In a blink they had passed it. Memories of the recent festivities at summer solstice, the rise of the longest day of the sun, and Heather's own spirit walk through the water, flashed by as Heather clung on.

After some time they came to a woodland. The Messenger Unicorn gently slowed down to a trot then a walk.

Heather, exhausted, leant forward onto her mane, "Why are you glowing?"

"You'll see," replied the Messenger in her horsey way, "At the edge of these trees are the Glowing Caves, whatever enters here, leaves here glowing like a star, until the glow wears off and falls like dust. We'll have to go through, this is the only way to our herd."

"There's many more of you?" asked Heather. She wanted to ask about the stories of unicorns she'd heard, but found her mouth shut tight and afraid to ask; what if they were true?

"Yes there are many of us now, we were on the brink of extinction." The Messenger turned her majestic head back to look at Heather. "In the past your kind hunted us down, we'll never trust a fully grown man-thing...," her voice trailed off

16

and she turned her head back to the way ahead.

"I'm a girl!" said Heather indignantly.

"Same thing," said the Messenger, "born of man and woman... yet, yes... not the same, not full grown, not yet thoughts and deeds set in mind. And I can sense your soul is good."

Heather, getting braver, "Why did they hunt you?"

"For our horns. They are magic." The Messenger plodded on, the trees thinned and beyond them you could see a faint glow coming from the rocks ahead. "And now something else hunts us...."

"What?" Heather asked anxiously.

Distantly, the Messenger continued, "Yes, and we can not defeat them alone...."

"Them?" asked Heather, more anxiously.

They were now at the edge of the trees. The unicorn paused, she lifted her head and sniffed the air to the left and to the right. Carefully she walked out of the trees then trotted across the clearing towards the rocks and into the entrance of the Glowing Caves.

"...One beast lives here. Here in these caves," continued the Messenger Unicorn.

Heather let out a stifled shriek.

"Don't be alarmed," the unicorn nickered, rather blase, "we won't pass by his lair."

Then, she added more seriously, "His name is the Beast of Thoemanny. He stands tall, like a giant man, but his hair is thick all over his body, two horns grow out of his head like an aurochs, and scales and spikes along his back like the dragons of long ago. We believe he is the last of his kind, we would leave him alone, but that he has taken a liking to young unicorns' blood.... It was rumoured he took a young man-thing too." Heather's hair on the back of her neck bristled.

Every sound echoed around them as they stepped through the tunnels of the Glowing Caves. The caves were vast, huge chambers with great columns supporting them like stone trees, with many tunnels leading off in different directions. A strange bright lichen trailed down and spread over the rock walls. Heather reached out and touched a piece and found it covered in a bright yellow glowing dust which was strangely warm and came off on her fingers. She wiped her fingers behind her on the unicorn's back.

They came to an underground river, the Messenger Unicorn explained how it grew and shrunk, raged and diminished, and was forever changing its shape and force within a few hours. It was to be respected. They waded in, the swirling water came up to Heather's thighs, it was cold, despite the warmth of the caves, and glistened in the strange golden glow, sending spiral patterns on the walls of the rock above them. They climbed out and up the small bank on the other side, the tunnel ahead of them was darker, the glow fading. They remained alert for all noises of any other cave occupants and steadily went down the tunnel.

It led to outside, it was just before dawn. Still dark enough to see the glowing dusty trail from the Messenger Unicorn's hooves. Heather looked down at her arms and realised she was glowing too.

"Just down here is our valley, my herd is here, my brothers, sisters and friends," the Messenger softly nickered. "I will take you to see the King."

They picked their way down through the bilberries and bracken, then the path opened out onto a grand valley, the sun was sending its first rays of light across the grassy plain, gently moving in the breeze. There, many unicorns were grazing peacefully, it was truly beautiful.

Heather dismounted and stood rather wobbly from the long ride. She walked alongside the Messenger Unicorn through the long waves of grass. A gentle rain wetted her face. A slate coloured stallion lifted his great head up from grazing. He shook his mane and Heather looked on in awe. The sunlight caught his mane like silver, his horn was pale golden, perfect and powerful, his grey body solid and strong, glistening in the light rain and early sunlight. From either side, two magnificent wings grew, which he opened wide and spread like an eagle.

The Messenger bowed, "My King."

"Messenger," the King lowered his head, and added enquiringly, "you found a young man-thing?"

"Girl!" interrupted Heather, "and my name's Heather."

The King moved his gaze across to her and tilted his head. "So, you're going to help us?"

Heather, hesitantly boldly, "er, y-yes?"

"You've come this far, it takes courage, curiosity and nerve to ride one of us," the King continued. "You know why we need your help?"

"No, well," Heather paused, "something to do with a beast or beasts? But how can I help you?"

"Yes, it is a grave situation. Something is taking our young unicorns and mares. There were two beasts, the Beast of Thoemanny and the Beast of Dekserot, they started taking our young colts and fillies ...to eat." The King's eyes were deep and serious.

"We tried to move our herd further down the valley, but we were caught between the two, the Beast of Dekserot lived in the Forests of Eagla in the foothills of The Mountains of Falling Stones, over there," he gestured with his head towards the vast mountain range at the far end of the valley. "And the

19

Beast of Thoemanny, has the Messenger told you about him? He has his lair in The Glowing Caves." He looked across at the Messenger.

"Yes," the Messenger shook her head in sorrow and took up the story. "Next a couple of mares were taken. We looked for them for days but could find no trace, of neither the beasts nor the unicorns. They must be well hidden, they could be dead or worse, kept alive for the beasts to feed on through the coming winter. It's so awful."

Tears welled up in her eyes as she continued, "Then I was walking through the Glowing Caves returning from searching when both beasts jumped out at me. I was terrified, I kicked violently and broke Thoemanny's leg and chased Dekserot out of the caves and into the Mountains of Falling Stones. There a giant falling stone hit him and pushed him down a cliff. He must have fallen to his death."

The King interjected, "But, be it beast or man, something or things is still taking our unicorns. Slowly, silently, one by one we are getting less and less. You have to help us. We've been fearful of your kind for too long now. It's time for change. Here we're hunted by beasts, move closer to man-things and we're hunted for our horns, that has to change. I've heard Thoemanny has taken a young man-thing too. Do your people know of these beasts? Had you heard of them? Have you noticed any of your kind disappearing? Does your tribe still go out to hunt us?"

Heather felt a passion rise up inside her. "We know the tales of old. Of, of... unicorns... taking deer, a dog too, and a child, seven hundred ages of the moon ago. I'm sorry." She looked down, ashamed at the stories she'd been told and how hated unicorns were amongst her people.

The King neighed emphatically, "All animals are loyal to

20

us! We would not hurt them! We would not hurt the man-things, except... when they hunt us!"

Heather felt small, fearful and white.

The King and the Messenger turned their heads to each other and exchanged soft whinnies.

The Messenger felt sorry for her. "Would you like to look around? When the rain's stopped I'll take you through our valley, and beyond, to the Mountains of Falling Stones."

Heather climbed back upon the Messenger's back, who then bowed her head to the King.

The King whinnied, "Thank you Messenger, the 'girl' needs to know the land and on your return we'll hold council with the elders."

The Messenger and Heather stopped to eat at a crab apple tree, which had dropped most of its apples after a storm, and drank from a small stream running near by. The rain had stopped and they then walked off down the valley.

III

THE MOUNTAINS OF FALLING STONES

At the far end of the valley the land started to rise up, boulders were strewn about interspersed with trees. Heather and the Messenger picked their way through, steadily upwards as the trees thickened, venturing deeper into the forest. It was much cooler under the heavy shade of the trees, and darker, Heather, still quite nervous about what she was now involved in, started to wish for home.

They climbed higher and higher, threading through the trees, following a thin, little used trail. Tree boughs bent and twisted across their path, the birds that sang at the beginning of the forest were quiet now, making their steps echo in the silence. The shadows grew darker and Heather felt uneasy. She was hungry too, the apples hadn't filled her up and it must be mid morning by now, and she had no provisions with her.

"How far are we going?" she asked.

The Messenger shook her soft mane, "We'll be out of the trees soon, we're going to climb to the top of this mountain. This is the start of the Mountains of Falling Stones, it can be perilous here so it's important I show you which way to go. From the top we can see all around for miles."

The echoey silence of the thick trees continued as they rose higher still. Eventually the top branches broke the quiet as the wind blew through them, rustling their leaves and cracking their twigs. The trees thinned and grew smaller, the land became rockier and dryer, and it was noticeably colder.

Then they were out of the trees, the land fell away to either side of them, far down to the right it rolled out like a blanket of green moss, to the left it crumbled and cracked like the scar a stone axe leaves on a tree stump. These mountains were young, they were walking along a ridge which led up to the peak, in the distance a volcano rumbled and smoked. The ridge got quite narrow, stones fell away under the Messenger's hooves, but then widened out and they were at the top, the sun now high above them.

Many peaks spread out before them, bleached by the sun and dusty like chalk, jagged and angry as they jilted out of the earth. To the other side, beyond the wide sweeping valley of the unicorns, beyond the rocky outcrop that hid the Glowing Caves, lay the hills and lowlands of Heather's home. Heather dismounted, stretched and sat down to take in the panorama. She was in awe, it was quite beautiful in all its wild harshness.

Just then they heard a distant neigh.

Heather turned around. "What's that at the edge of the trees coming towards us? It looks like, like the King?"

The Messenger turned her head, lifted it and sniffed the

23

breeze, she whinnied, "Something's wrong." And she began a swift trot over the ridge, with Heather jogging behind, to meet the King Unicorn.

Galloping across to them at great speed, distressed and exhausted, the King called out to them once they were in earshot. "They're here, they've come again, BOTH terrible beasts! ...Rounded up the mares and foals!"

The Messenger and Heather rushed to him.

"I chased them, I kicked... knocked one down, but I was hit, by the other's great tails... knocked to the ground, cold. When I got up they had gone. They were working TOGETHER, communicating to each other! Thoemanny... with... this is greater than I'd feared... DEKSEROT! ...he lives!"

Fear rose up in the Messenger's eyes, "Where are the mares and foals? Have they all gone?"

"No," neighed the King, "Most got away. When I came to, I gathered together who was left, they were so frightened. I left the elders in charge while I came to find you."

The fear in the Messenger's eyes ignited her rage, "Get on my back," she commanded, and the three of them began the descent.

Sweating from their race downhill they stood together with the elders: an old black stallion, with silver wings and horn similar to the Kings, pawed the ground and swished his greying tail, eyeing up Heather suspiciously. Two mares, stood agitated, one a light silver grey and one a dun cream, both with light golden horns but no wings, also swished their tails, keeping time with the old stallion elder. Each bowed to the King.

The King began. "Any news of the taken ones since I've been gone? Has the search party returned?"

"No, sire," the silver mare solemnly replied. "The search

party has not yet returned."

"Then we must act," he continued. "We must move the rest of the herd down the valley, keep near the river and stay amongst the tall grasses and shrubs, keep hidden. You three stay there to watch over them." He shook his long mane. "Dekserot was presumed dead, now we know that he still lives. Him and Thoemanny appear to be working together, they spoke to each other in their language and moved like two dogs circling our young unicorns and mares. They drove them into the Forest of Eagla. Our search party took after them, if they're not back soon I shall go myself. We will not give up until we find them."

The other unicorns lifted their heads up in agreement.

The King continued, "Messenger, after we have moved the herd down to the other end of the valley you take the girl Heather back to her tribe. Then you must rest, you are starting to look heavy with foal, it will be due before not too long."

The Messenger looked to Heather.

The King carried on, "Heather, on your return to your tribe you must tell your elders of these beasts. It is important they believe you, to build trust between man-things and unicorns. You must prepare to defend yourselves against what may come. Gather your weapons, strengthen your watch, and wait for our return."

The King and the elders moved off, calling out to the rest of the herd that stood nervously nearby. At a quiet but fast pace they all cantered down the valley and entered the tall grasses, here they could find some cover. There was some grazing for the unicorns and water from the river.

It was now late afternoon, Heather got down off the Messenger's back and gathered berries from the blackberry briars close by, their sweet taste so good. Nearer the water's

25

edge she found some duck eggs, tapped a small hole in one end and hungrily sucked the contents.

The Messenger nickered and stopped. She hadn't stopped sweating. She pawed the ground and threw her head down and shook her mane then nipped at her flanks. She walked down to a small beach where the river was shallow and waded in cooling her legs. She sipped at the water, then walked out and over to the shade of an oak, pawing the ground. She turned around and lay down, only to get up again a few minutes later and do the same thing again. She stood up and nipped at her flanks again, a soft breeze lifted her pale golden mane and caused a shiver from her sweating coat. Her foal was coming.

Heather had been watching from a distance when the dun mare elder came up, "Her foal will come tonight. She won't be able to take you back just yet. Stay with me, she'll need peace and quiet, her own space. The beasts' attack and your race downhill has brought on her labour early."

The breeze picked up, thick grey clouds hung heavily over the far end of the rocky ridge that ran all the way down the length of the valley. Behind them at the other end of the band of rock was the Forest of Eagla, the way the beasts had driven the unicorns. Between the two lay the entrance to the Glowing Caves; Heather's way home, and Thoemanny's lair....

As the sky grew darker, a distant rumble of thunder echoed, answered by another further away. Next came a flash, a dart sending fingers of light across the sky. Heather huddled closer into the hollow in the tree roots she'd found for shelter, for the night and the coming rain, next to the dun mare. She still feared a storm, despite by her twelve years she could hunt, fish and look after herself.

The rain fell. Through the breaks in the fleeing clouds the full moon shone. In the distance the thunder crashed and the lightning continued to spit across the sky.

And then the storm was gone. Heather looked out, she hadn't slept well. Over by a small oak she saw the Messenger and she wasn't alone, nuzzled close to her belly lay a beautiful foal, perfect and silver in the moonlight. She walked over to them, far away the dark clouds rolled taking their thunder and the last few sparks of lightning chasing after.

Carefully she knelt down beside them, the Messenger moved her gracious head towards Heather and her beautiful eyes met hers. The little foal raised its head and its big eyes stared brightly back.

"Isn't he handsome?" she nickered, "he can be yours to ride when he's grown. He will be fine and fast. He won't follow me and be a messenger, only mares and fillies can be a messenger unicorn. You can name him if you like?"

Heather stroked his soft muzzle and forehead where a small bump of a horn bud grew, she mused on a name to call such a beautiful baby creature that would grow into something quite majestic.

"Spear.... Spike... no." She looked at the ebbing storm clouds, then back to the foal. His smooth coat was a dark golden, his pale golden mane stuck up all fluffy and new. One last flash of lightning spat across the distant sky, like kindling spits fire, the little spit of fire mirrored in his deep blue eyes.

And it came to her, "I'll name him Spit Fire," she said.

"Spit Fire," echoed the Messenger, and they sat together for the rest of the night, taking comfort in each other's warmth, till sleep softly took them.

The morning was fresh, Heather awoke late, the Messenger and her foal were a short way off, Spit Fire was suckling from his mother as she grazed. After collecting and eating a breakfast of leaves and fruit Heather went down to the river and washed her arms and face, walking back up the bank she met the Messenger and Spit Fire grazing at the top. The foal lifted his head from suckling and pranced about testing his legs. He stopped for a moment and looked straight at her, Heather was amazed to see that his horn had grown to almost the size of her thumb, doubling in size since last night. He looked stronger and more sturdy already, yet only still a few hours old.

The ancient fireside tales, her uncle told them when they were young, came back to her. Of unicorns and their magic, how a youngling unicorn could grow so fast, being tall and strong enough to defend itself in a few weeks. How a young colt could be so terrifying as to compare to the strength of two aurochs and could kill a dragon from long ago. How no man or woman had ever got close to a living unicorn, except to hunt it down and take its precious enchanted horn. No unicorn had ever been tamed, or touched, let alone ridden, they were too wild, too shy, too elusive, too dangerous and too feared. Their horns were said to kill and to cure, sacred properties that held true even after taken from a dead unicorn. Her uncle had passed one around, fragile and intact, its intricate spiralling and dulled silver-grey hue, was no comparison to the horns on the living unicorns that Heather had met. They were alive, and not dead. Alive, as they should be.

The search party had not returned that night, and so the King had gone after them. Two days passed until he returned with the party, and they had not found the unicorns that were taken. A sad air hung over them all. They kept to the river's edge, hidden in the long grasses, they all remained on high alert but there was no sound or sight of the beasts.

Several days passed by while Heather stayed with the unicorns. She walked with the Messenger and Spit Fire as he grew and grew each day, talking and learning of their ways, each exchanging stories of their cultures and customs.

The sun rose and the sun set, again and again.

She whittled a long stick with a flint and hand wove twine from gathered nettles, binding her hands with her scarf to avoid the stings. She gathered fruit, leaves, fresh river mussels and snails to eat, and eggs from the birds and ducks that nested near the water. But she grew hungry for deer roasted over a crackling fire that her family and tribe would share. For duck, deer-milk, honey and sweet-breads that her mother made. For her own bed of ferns and furs, for the times she chased her sister with a game of shooting berries through a hollow reed. For the comfort of her mother, the protection of her father, the warmth of a fire. She hadn't lit a fire here for fear of drawing attention to where they hid. She missed home.

The seventh day was drawing in, when the King approached. "It is time. The Messenger's foal is grown enough now to follow his mother when she takes you home. Remember what I said. You must gain the trust of your elders to work with us to fight these beasts. We will not give up on the lost ones. We will find them. But it will mean us coming out of our valley and meeting with man-things," a snort of disgust.... "We can not risk that if we are to be hunted again. You understand? And these beasts will not stop at unicorn blood...."

Heather nodded. She ran down to where the Messenger and Spit Fire were grazing, not able to contain her excitement. "You can take me home?!"

The Messenger bowed her head, nuzzled Spit Fire at her flank, and nickered, "Let's go."

They went quietly and cautiously through the Glowing Caves, ears pricked, eyes wide, nostrils flared, horns tingling, all senses alert. A unicorn's horn is highly sensitive, like a third eye. Spit Fire's horn now stood the span of Heather's hand above his forehead, covered in a velvety fine hair twisting up to a fine point. Their hooves tapped on, over the dusty rocky floor, out of the tunnel and into the grand chamber where the ever changing river passed. Crossing that they hurried on, well aware that although no trace of the beasts had been found since they attacked the herd, they were still close to Thoemanny's lair.

And then they were outside, relieved to be through the caves. They picked up pace to a fast canter.

Over hills, crossing streams, through the lowlands and oak and hazel woodlands, they were nearing home. Heather gripped the Messenger's mane anxiously, she'd lost track of how many days she'd been gone, though her parents trusted her out on a trek, being gone several days was different. She didn't know how they would react.

Heather looked at the moon, its height in the sky told her it was very early in the morning, maybe she could sneak back into their cave without being noticed? The unicorns stayed in the shadows and she dismounted. Feeling a mixture of emotions to be home, doubt crept into her thoughts, would they believe her? That the unicorns were ally and not foe? Heather stood a while looking on at her home.

"Good luck," neighed the Messenger. "Await our return, till then, goodbye." She turned to say goodbye to the unicorns, but with a flash of their tails they were gone. She was alone.

Spit Fire

IV

THE WATCHER'S
CAVE

The wattle hazel door stood fast, and no amount of shoving would budge it. Heather looked back and called out softly to the unicorns, but they were gone already. She leant back against the door and decided to wait till morning rose.

Cold and sleepy the hours dragged. Heather, fed up of waiting, decided to throw a rock at the doorway and rattle the door to wake them up.

The gruff half asleep voice of her father stirred inside....

She called out. "Is anyone awake?"

"Heather!" came her father's deep voice.

"Heather?" came her mother's softer voice.

The door was thrust aside and she was pulled quickly inside.

"You're alive!" shrieked her mother, weeping. "Thank the gods!" And gathered her up in her protective arms.

"Where've you been?" said her father sternly, and to her mother, "It's nothing to do with the gods."

Heather just looked on, she wanted to explain, but nothing came out.

"She'd a' been at the village over the river, I'm sure," continued her father as she didn't answer. "And up to no good at that. What with all these goings on, worrying us sick."

Olga, her sister, had woken too. She ran up to her and hugged her.

"Three deer were taken," Heather's mother began. "They found hoof prints and broken branches, scored bark on the trees... they say it's unicorns!"

"There's no unicorns now, they've been extinct for ages!" argued her father.

"Well what's taken our deer? And what's next? Our children?" her mother retorted. "I thought they'd taken you...," her eyes welled up again.

"I'll go and find whoever and wherever you've been, and show them what for!" Heather's father stomped about the cave looking for something.

The commotion continued, Heather still couldn't speak. Her mother stirred the embers of the fire, her father grabbed his stone axe and stormed out without a word.

Heather's father was a sombre man. Fit, agile, thick and toned, his dark hair fell over his broad shoulders and he wore his beard in a plait. The mark of the strong white stag, the Trosban, the mark of their tribe, was etched into the skin of his chest now faded and blue. An ink mixed from charcoal and woad, tapped in with a fine bone, flax swab and stone tapper.

"Thank the gods, thank the gods, you're safe." Heather's

mother placed a small round rock into the fire. "To Duer, god of water, thank you." Placing another stone into the hearth, she recited to the awakening flames, "to Taiu, god of fire, to Daearh, goddess of earth, and to Gwynt, goddess of the wind, we thank you." And she placed two more stones into the fire. She threw a shawl of russet linen, madder dyed, loosely round her shoulders and sat back looking at the fire.

Heather remained silent, watching her. Her mother was a slim woman, yet deceptively strong, her hair, a battleaxe red in the light of the fire. Four feathered plaits hung long and loose and dressed the sides of her face against her long hair; a mark of her past, her tribe of origin, the Iolaires, the eagles, but now taken by the Trosban, she was one of them.

Days passed.

And the unicorns didn't return.

And Heather didn't tell anyone about her adventures.

She went along with her father's assumption that she'd been off with the rival tribe across the water. How would they believe she'd ridden a unicorn? Sat with one and her new born foal? That they could speak? That there was a whole herd of them and that they meant her own people no harm and wanted their help in the fight against terrifying beasts? Her tribe believed it was unicorns taking the deer, they'd want her to show them where they lived to hunt them down. And now they had more reason to hate the neighbours over the water, they believed they'd lied about Heather staying there when her father asked far and wide of her whereabouts. Heather didn't know what to do for the best, maybe she should confide in her sister? She lay awake mulling it over and longing for the unicorns to return, for another adventure....

That night the strange glow appeared again. Heather, a light sleeper, woke and crept across the floor. The hazel door had been wedged tightly shut with a large branch on the inside, as quietly as she could she moved the wedge and eased open the door ajar.

There stood Spit Fire. Glowing and stunning, he'd grown again. Next to him stood the Messenger, both drenched in the golden light.

The Messenger pawed the ground, "Did you tell them? Will they help us?"

Heather slipped outside and pulled the hazel door to behind her, "Not yet," she said. "They won't believe me. There's been some trouble with deer being taken, they found trampled bushes and hoof marks. They think unicorns have taken them. I won't be allowed to go out again... I'm not the one to help you." She sank her head, "I'm so sorry."

The unicorns shook their heads and manes. The Messenger spoke again, "Solas, the dun mare elder warned of this." Mother and son looked at each other and snorted.

"What now?" asked Spit Fire.

The Messenger replied with a toss of her mane, she turned her head, about to leave. "We go. We're on our own." Then looking back to Heather. "If we get attacked by man-things when we extend our search for the lost unicorns, we *will* fight back."

She paused, sadness in her eyes, and gave Heather a look that seemed to penetrate her soul. They turned to go.

Just then the hazel door jerked and creaked against the weight of something leaning on it on the other side. They all looked around. Slowly the door opened more and Olga pushed her head out, awe in her eyes at the sight before her.

"Olga!" exclaimed Heather.

"I heard everything," Olga said, straightening her soft woven tunic to join Heather on the ground. "I was watching and listening since you first moved the branch away from the door. Unicorns! Wow! Amazing!"

The unicorns stopped, they turned back around and faced the girls.

Heather got up and threw her arms round Spit Fire's neck, she nuzzled her face into his soft neck, "Don't go!"

He bent his head round to nuzzle her and blew a soft agreement through his nostrils.

"This is Spit Fire, and this is the Messenger. My friends. And they need our help."

The Messenger whinnied. "Yes."

"I wasn't at the village over the water. I was with these unicorns all that time," began Heather. And she and the unicorns proceeded to tell Olga everything.

"Maybe we can still work together," the Messenger neighed. "Get on my back, both of you," she said to Heather and Olga in her horsey way, and to Spit Fire, "Come on. We'll show them our valley, our King and our plight. We'll show them the lie of the land, the dangers and where to go. We can't give up the search for the lost unicorns." And she stamped her hoof.

Heather and Olga obediently climbed up onto her broad back.

"Hold onto me," said Heather to Olga, gripping the Messenger's mane. The unicorns gave a small rear and they galloped off into the night.

They galloped across the hills to the Glowing Caves, taking a cautious way through the tunnels and on to the unicorn's valley. They were going at a slower pace than before and Heather tried to memorize the way they took.

Olga, younger than Heather by three years, and quite a capable rider, was fascinated and enthralled by the adventure. She accepted the unicorns talking like it was quite natural and never questioned their reasons to need their help. She shared Heather's passion in wanting to help, being three years younger she hadn't been initiated in the art of hunting and in her innocence she was courageous.

They met with the King and the elders in a dry clearing near the rock face. A rough map was etched out in the dusty ground. The areas they'd searched were drawn out, and the areas they hadn't covered, the King scraped out with his hoof. These were the areas the Messenger was to search.

Addressing the Messenger, the King spoke. "You can take the girls along to help you in your search. I will only send you, as we don't want to draw attention to ourselves in the land of the man-things. We don't want to be seen and we don't want to lead any things back to our valley."

"Heather, Olga, do you think the deer disappearing from your home is the work of the beasts?" the King asked.

"I'm not sure, I don't see how they could both have got near to our village without being seen," Heather replied, looking across at Olga.

Olga shrugged her shoulders, "So what do these beasts look like?"

The old grey stallion, Samant, the elder, spoke up. "Thoemanny stands tall like a giant man-thing. Covered in hair and spiked scales down his back, with two great curved horns growing out of the sides of his head. His face is wrinkled and aged, he is old, the last of his kind. He has quite an appetite for meat, with claws and teeth that can rip you apart. And now we've seen him working together with Dekserot, the last of the dragoss."

The silver mare elder continued, "Dekserot is a beast similar to the dragons of old. He walks on all fours with two great tails that can knock down a tree. His body is long with scales on his back and spikes on his spine, he has puny wings that don't allow him to really fly, but vicious, vicious fangs, and the same liking for meat, unicorn meat...." her voice trailed off.

Olga shuddered.

"We should get back before sunrise," Heather said reaching out for Olga's hand. The two sisters looked at each other, their faces gone pale.

The King carried on, "Yes, we'll carry you home, we don't want to raise any more suspicion. But you'll help us in the search. We will come for you. And back at your village, try to find out what your elders plan to do, as they believe us unicorns are to blame for the attack on the deer. It could be the beasts. Keep alert. Keep safe."

The Messenger took Heather and Olga on her back, Spit Fire followed behind, back through the tunnels and labyrinths of the Glowing Caves. They set off for the hills of Heather and Olga's home, taking a longer, different route along the outskirts of the Forest of Eagla that fell either side of the ridgeway that ran along the unicorn's valley. They searched for signs of the lost unicorns, a trail, a hoof mark, a strand of hair, but found nothing. Thick ancient forest lay like a blanket for miles and miles, boar trotted through the trees, stopping now and again to nudge in the undergrowth, keeping their distance from the travellers.

As they followed the Great River towards the girls' village, the trees thinned and wild deer flitted through the shadows. It was almost dawn. In the growing light, you could just make out the huts of their village in the distance, thin lazy trails of smoke drifting up into the deep lilac clouds stretched across the sky.

V

THE BEAST OF BAS

The elders had gathered in the hall, a large round structure of wooden poles with a steeply sloping thatch roof that reached almost to the ground. Sitting cross-legged round a fire pit, the head of the Trosban tribe, the Chief, passed a bowl of barley whisky to the elder to his left. The bowl was carved out of bone and intricately decorated. The elder drank solemnly.

The Chief stood up, his hair pulled back high on his head in a twisted knot, his greying beard, long and plaited, the lines on his face told of his years and experience. He surveyed the gathering in the hall of elders and watchers, and took his long staff, pounding it on the hard earth three times, he then spoke, "More hoof prints were found last night. Near the watchers' caves. Ethlemore returning from the deer woodland, reports our deer are untouched. But that they are unsettled."

The bowl was passed from elder to elder.

Greyla, a woman, bent of many years, whispered, "Unicorns...."

39

Rumblings went around the room. Some disputing this theory, some in agreement. Some disputing unicorns existence, some laying blame on them for all their ills.

The Chief drove his staff down into the ground again, four more times.

"Unicorns," he repeated. "It could be. The old paintings at the Sacre Ogof tell the stories of old when there were many. They killed us back then. They will kill us again! The only thing that can protect us is a horn from the very beast." He gripped the long spiral unicorn horn held by a strap of leather tied round his neck and lifted it over his head.

"This...." He held it up. And placed a glowing chunk of birch resin into the herbs that were crushed inside it. It began to smoke. "Will give us the sight we need." Bringing the smoking horn up to his face, he took a long deep breath in. His eyes rolled back and the man to his left reached for the horn as he loosened his grip. They each inhaled deeply as the horn was passed ceremoniously between them.

"There are more of them.... They will take two of our children!" moaned Greyla, possessed.

There was a lull of silence, then the Chief spoke in a trance, "There's a dragon too...."

And out of the fire rose up a great ball of flames and an unearthly roar... splitting the flames apart and opening into a savage jaw jammed with jagged teeth....

These had been relatively peaceful times. The watchers' caves on the edge of the village had relaxed their watch. Marauding tribes from across the river had ceased attacking long ago, and trade begun again, bringing skills, tools and produce. The Trosban tribe kept a few small subsistence farms while still maintaining their hunter gatherer traditions, and deer were managed in the woodlands close beside their village, little undisturbed until now.

The elders sent men out tracking, Odhar, Heather and Olga's father, amongst them. They'd found a few more hoof marks leading away in the direction of the Mountains of Falling Stones, (that the villagers called the Crumbling Mountains) but that was all. No one ever ventured that far for fear of dragons from the tales of long ago.

A whole moon rose and fell till it was whole again and the unicorns did not come.

Heather and Olga sat in a clearing in the village centre twisting and moulding clay. Next to them breathed and scorched, with intense heat, a charcoal fire, in a pit dug into the earth. They were making bowls with the other children, all ages joining in. Bowls that had dried out for a few days were placed into the pit with long sticks to be fired.

The clay in Olga's hand didn't look like a bowl. It began to take the form of a small animal. As she smoothed the silky clay with her fingers, she closed her eyes and imagined the unicorns. When she opened them she looked down at what she'd made and lying in her palm was a little unicorn foal. Showing Heather but hiding it so as not to show the others, she ran off back towards their cave. On her way she passed men carrying large poles of wood, these they were driving into the ground in front of the ramparts around their village to strengthen their defences. Some of the older boys were helping, one a few years older than Olga, yet tall and strong for his age, carried a log with ease on his shoulder. Olga disliked this boy, Brae. He was training to be a watcher and had received his first tattoo, an eagle on his chest. And he strutted his position only too well.

41

On seeing Olga running he stopped, blocking her way, laughing and not letting her pass. She stopped abruptly, dropping the unicorn. Brae looked down at the little clay shape lying misshapen in the mud, jeering at her he went to kick it, but Olga grabbed it up.

"You should have a boar tattooed on your chest, not an eagle!" she challenged, and ran on, Brae shouting something after her.

She carried on to their home, relieved to be inside, and in the centre of the room the fire still glowed. She carefully placed the clay unicorn into the embers and covered it with hot ash.

That night Heather lay tossing and turning in her sleep, locked deep within a dream. She was riding Spit Fire, riding like the wind, beautiful, exciting, then the dream quickly changed. Suddenly they were being chased by a huge tiger, running and running through an endless barren land. They stopped and could go no more, the tiger snarled baring all its fangs, then grew and changed, morphing into a giant beast that Heather had never seen or heard of before. It was huge, like the size of the great dragon bones they'd found at the Sacre Ogof, much bigger than the Beast of Thoemanny or the Beast of Dekserot. And larger than the great elephants or mammoths that lived when ice gripped the world. It kept the tiger's stripes, which stretched as it grew, but its back became arched growing menacing spikes, a curved horn grew out of its head and blood dripped from its nose and mouth. It came right up close to Heather's face and opened its jaws... and inside, lying on its wet, blood soaked tongue, was the small clay unicorn Olga had made....

Heather awoke with a start, her heart thumping in her chest. Relieved to find it was just a dream she lay back down and breathed, pulling her fur skins up around her chin, she felt suddenly cold. She lay with her eyes open a while to reassure herself everything was normal, then turned on her side and closed her eyes, though she could not sleep again.

In the morning, sitting outside in the early sun, she told Olga about her dream. She worried about what it could mean.

"It was so real, I think we should tell the unicorns," said Heather, in a tone of urgency. "What if it's something to do with the missing unicorns?"

"We tell them when they come," replied Olga, "it's been a long time now, they must be coming again soon?"

"I can't just leave it, I feel I must tell them," worried Heather.

"Look, I don't know, I think we should wait," urged Olga.

They continued to argue, getting louder and louder.

Their mother came out, chastising them for the noise and asked them to help with her weaving, which they did reluctantly.

"We'll need some berries and weld for this next lot," she muttered, "a good skin full."

"I'll go!" said Heather, jumping at the opportunity. Neither her nor Olga had been further than their village woodlands since their last trip with the unicorns. Four weeks on and the tribe was relaxing a little, though work on their defence wall remained constant and the watchers continued their vigil.

Their mother paused, and took a long look from Heather to Olga, "Well take this," she handed Olga a spear and Heather an axe and a deerskin bag. "Take some eggs and sweet-bread and be back before dusk."

Freedom.

It was good to leave the hustle of the village behind them and escape, run and practise throwing the spear and axe.

43

Forgetting their argument earlier, they laughed and chased each other through the dappled woodland. Down and through the pool at the base of the waterfall, splashing through small streams and forgetting their errand.

They came to the Sacre Ogof, the old sacred caves, sacred for their ancient cave art. Heather stood in the cool shade of the entrance. She touched the cave walls where huge paintings danced their story along the long length of the cave. Their colours of ochre, madder, chalk, charcoal and woad, no longer vibrant as the day they were painted, told a story of long ago. A scattering of deer began the tale, leaping across the stream-like veins in the rock, led by a great white stag. Wild boar and aurochs followed, then mammoths, giant elks, bears and lions, that roamed the land before the ice, grazing across the meadows of rock. A group of men and women held spears with arms raised high, in pursuit of seven unicorns galloping across the stone hills before them. The last unicorn stood still with wings outstretched wide and held its horn upwards to the sky. A faint image of another unicorn danced above, reaching up towards a painted star, with shining rays that spread out, up and across the cave ceiling and rained down on the whole scene like dew.

"It still amazes me," said Heather.

"Yes," agreed Olga, "it's beautiful."

"Look at the unicorns, and the people, it doesn't look like they're hunting them, more like they're praising them? Don't you think?" queried Heather. The girls stood in adoration of the ancient paintings for a while longer, forgetting the time, then ambled outside and wandered down through the woods.

They found themselves at the edge of the trees, lowland heath reached out in front of them, and they could see the tall yellow heads of the weld just above the bobbing grasses.

Running into the meadow they fell about rolling and laughing.

Heather stopped her play and became serious. "I could go now to the unicorns. It's not that far from here, I could make it."

Olga's smile dropped, and she paused. "*We* could make it." she said, and smiled at her sister.

The two girls, once unanimous in their decision, set off at a steady jog, excitement in the air.

It was further than they thought, it took them all day to reach the entrance of the Glowing Caves. Now they were there they were committed to their cause. They'd be better to reach the unicorns now anyway, for if they had to walk back from here they'd never make it back by nightfall, whereas if they could ride back on the unicorns, they would have time.

The caves welcomed them with their yellow glow. Heather and Olga walked inside, careful to go as quietly as they could. They came to the great chamber where a maze of tunnels led out, Heather felt sure she knew the way. It was the tunnel on the right, or straight ahead? She reached down and held Olga's hand and they walked on down, twisting and turning, on and on. She gripped Olga's hand tighter. They could hear their own breathing getting quicker and quicker, hearts racing, ears straining. It was a very long tunnel, just as Heather was starting to think they were lost, the tunnel began to widen out and it looked familiar, although they hadn't reached the underground river yet. The tunnel widened more, a vast crack in the rock opened above them, going way up high, she thought she could hear running water, she relaxed a little, maybe they were on the right path.... Then a clawed hand took hold of her shoulder!

Heather cried out in terror.

Olga screamed.

The Beast of Thoemanny let out a tremendous growl!

Olga, still holding Heather's hand, pulled her, trying to run ahead in the other direction, but coming down the tunnel in front of them was the Beast of Dekserot!

Thoemanny growled a gnarled dialect, and Dekserot drummed a guttural reply back.

Thoemanny dragged Heather and pushed Olga ahead of him towards Dekserot, she stumbled, she fell, her spear dropped, she tried to run, but they were trapped. There was no time to think, Dekserot backed off up the tunnel with Thoemanny pushing and dragging the girls ahead, they were caught between the two beasts.

Then they were outside. Heat, concentrated from the day, hit them. The tunnel led to an opening they hadn't used with the unicorns, to a place they'd not been to, a rocky dry place, they must be nearer the Mountains of Falling Stones, and the sun was slipping behind the far rocks.

And then Heather gasped in horror, ...there, standing heavily, shuffling its almighty weight from one foreleg to the other, tail sweeping a great arc in the dust behind its bulk, solid and massive, ...was the beast from her dream!

Olga broke away. She turned on Thoemanny, attacking his arm that held Heather, with teeth and nails, like a devil possessed. He shook her down. She got up. He shook her down again. In that moment, she realised her attempts were futile. And she watched on in pathetic horror.

Thoemanny pushed Heather against a rock, and moved another, grating over the rubble, up against her legs so she was ensnared.

Heather, beyond fear, shut her eyes and chanted to herself, the old words, the old chants, to the ancient gods of fire and ice, in the ancient tongue, *"briseadh crag, briseadh crag, briseadh suar, briseadh suar,"* ~ *'break these rocks, break these* rocks, break me free, break me free....'

Dekserot prowled in front of her, taunting the giant beast, like they were playing a game.

Thoemanny, gravelled a tone of deliverance.

Olga could watch no more.

She ran back to the shelter of the caves, her spear? Where was her spear? She had to help her sister! She ran full pelt a short way back the way they had come. Grabbed her fallen spear and the axe, and ran back to try to free Heather, dodging the beasts who were now fixated on the giant beast, taunting it with their game. Behind them she tugged at the smaller rock wedging Heather's legs, she tried levering it with the axe, it was no good, she couldn't move it enough in the time she had. She hugged her sister.

"If they take you, they take me too." Olga clung onto Heather, she gave her the axe. "We'll go down fighting."

That night Spit Fire had gone to the girls' cave. He had grown much bigger now, standing tall like a yearling, in only a few weeks. He had waited a long time but no Heather or Olga came out, no one came out. He sensed something was wrong. So he had returned to the valley and asked his mother, the Messenger, if she would go with him and look for them. She was with the rest of the herd, watching over the new young foals.

"I can't just now, wait till morning and I'll come with you?" she nickered.

"Something is very wrong, I feel it," Spit Fire replied.

The Messenger looked into her son's eyes, not sensing the same urgency that he did, distracted by the young foals.

"Tonight I'm watching the foals, I'll join you in the morning, if you wait till then?" She swished her tail and tossed her mane.

But Spit Fire couldn't wait. "I'm going," he neighed and turned and cantered off back towards the Glowing Caves.

Trotting fast he crossed the ever changing river and took the tunnel that led to Thoemanny's lair. The beasts were presumed to have moved on as no-one had heard or seen them since their attack.

Thoemanny's lair had been visited in their search for the unicorns, it had been found deserted, blood stains on the walls, old bones in the dust and two young unicorn horns cast aside. It wasn't a place they wished to re-visit.

Cautiously Spit Fire moved down the tunnel. He came to the lair. He looked about, nostrils flared, it smelt strongly of stale damp hair and excrement, Thoemanny! He'd been here recently. Spit Fire ventured on, beyond the lair, down another tunnel that he knew led higher up into the mountains. His senses tingling with adrenalin, he hurried on.

The beasts continued their game. Heather was the prize. Some kind of contest of bravado was taking place. Dekserot and Thoemanny biting the giant beast's legs and belly, and dodging the beast's blows as he swiped with his claws. Every so often they would all pause and rest, then their game would resume again. This had been going on for some time.

Heather, and Olga crouching down behind her, had been stealthily levering the rock with the axe. They found if they levered one side at a time its weight shifted and gave. Sliver by sliver it moved, both girls working together. And then she was free! Scrambling her legs out Heather made a run for the caves, Olga close behind her.

Dekserot had seen them, he roared.

Thoemanny, who was nearest, was onto them in two strides. He growled, baring his teeth, many wrinkles on his old face.

He caught Heather's leg. She fell. She cried out.

Olga reached out to fend him off.

The three of them caught in a desperate struggle.

Spit Fire broke out of the tunnel. Before him he saw the awful scene; Heather, Olga and Thoemanny. Dekserot too, baiting a much larger beast, one he'd not seen before.

He reared and neighed and charged over to them. Dekserot came at him, thundering. And the great beast close behind. Spit Fire reared at Thoemanny, he arched his neck to spear him, but Dekserot whacked his great tails round at him. Spit Fire missed. And ran a short way off to avoid their crushing blow. The giant beast roared and viciously nipped Dekserot and turned its great head towards Spit Fire, coming at him fast and making him back away towards the mountains.

In the fight they hadn't seen the great bird circling above. A wing span as wide as the King's outstretched wings. It dived. Dropping like a bomb amidst the struggle, and dug its talons deep into Thoemanny's arm.

Thoemanny roared and yelped. He dropped his grip on Heather's leg.

The great bird flew off.

Dekserot and the beast were still close by but Spit Fire rushed in. Dekserot faced him drawing his mouth back into a snarl, sucking in the air through his jagged teeth and spuing out a throw of flames across the dust.

Spit fire, unfaltering, charged across the carpet of flames to the girls. Thoemanny, who lay holding his wounded arm, roared and began to get up.

In that moment Olga grabbed hold of Heather and they both scrabbled onto Spit Fire's back.

He ran. Straight through the caves, both girls lying flat,

hugged close to his body, fleeing so fast, not caring if he scraped the rock walls as he flew down them.

Then they were out. Out in the valley. He carried on galloping, straight to the end of the valley where the half hidden herd were gathered.

"King, Sire...," he bowed, flanks heaving heavily, sweat running off his neck and back.

"There's another beast, a great beast, and Thoemanny, Dekserot! They were all there... they had the girls!" he panted. "A bird, a great bird, helped."

The girls, terrified but grateful for their sanctuary, still lay on his back, they slowly got down and began to recount their tale, right from where Heather dreamt about the beast.

The King paced the ground. The other unicorns had gathered round to hear what was going on.

The King continued, "Three beasts now threaten our herd." He stopped pacing and stretched his wings to their full span. "We have lost half our herd to them, we can not loose more. We confront them, we find where the lost unicorns are, we fight if we have to. All unicorns above a full circle of the moon in age will fight."

There was some whinnying and unrest amongst the gathered unicorns.

"This new beast, Heather," the King spoke again. "It came to you in a dream, a warning from the god of gods, you should name it."

There was a silence. The gods only spoke to some in dreams, but the god of gods?

Heather broke the silence. "It was so terrifying, like death, worse than the legends of the dragons before the ice. A beast of death, or to use the old word for death, *bas*, from the time of dragons, it should be known as the Beast of Bas."

And it was agreed, the name for the new beast, ...the Beast of Bas.

VI

DARK FIRE

The unicorns that were old enough to fight came forward, Spit Fire included, just a few mares would stay back to watch over the foals. They gathered round the King.

Then came a sound of distant hooves. All ears pricked forward towards the noise. It grew louder. Along with the sounds of the hooves came whinnies and neighs. In the distance, five unicorns came galloping across the valley. The King and the others rushed forward to greet them. Five young unicorns; three fillies and two colts, five of the lost, five of the taken ones. They welcomed them with whinnies of joy and everyone wanted to know what had happened, where they'd been taken, where were the others, were the others alive?

The young five told their story. After their capture they'd been taken to the mountains, to an inhospitable place, sparse of vegetation and few trees, on one side a cliff edge, tall shear rock on the other and only one way out. Here they'd been watched by each of the three beasts, hidden away, surviving on the few bits of grass and thorns they could find. Each week a unicorn would be taken away and not return.

They had heard the screams and the fighting and had ventured out of their captivity. They had seen Spit Fire, a new unicorn, taking two man-things on his back, Thoemanny lying injured, Dekserot and the Beast of Bas fighting each other and a great bird flying away. They all had tried to run, but Dekserot breathed a curtain of fire to stop them, only the five made it back to the herd.

The herd were noisy. All eager to hear which unicorns were still alive.

Spit Fire turned to Heather, "I sense danger."

With all the noise from the returning unicorns no one noticed the smoke. He lifted his head, nostrils flared. "It smells like... smoke, ...fire, *FIRE*!" And looking back, from the mountains there rose up a great funnel of thick smoke.

The King started forward, neighing, "Quick, we go now to find the rest of the herd, before the fire gets too great. We go straight down our valley to the mountains, the five can lead the way."

Heather jumped on Spit Fire, and Olga on the Messenger and they charged ahead, along with a strong band of unicorns, towards the mountains and the fire.

But the fire had grown too big, the dry land had ignited fast, spreading the fire at an alarming rate. Birds left the canopy of the trees, flying and screeching as they fled the smoke. Deer and wild cats ran together, past them, terror in their eyes. All the animals of the forest were fleeing the flames.

The unicorns cautiously carried on, until they were met by a wall of intense heat and crackling tall trees encompassed with flames, and they could go no further.

They halted and watched on. A horrible roaring, a deep bellowing groan, came from deep within the fire. Through the flames and smoke ahead of them, they could make out the shape of a great beast, the Beast of Bas... Its great head was thrown back, reaching up, its throat bulging and pulsing as it roared. The trees grew closer together here lower down the mountain, and it couldn't escape the encircling flames as the fire had spread downhill after it. They watched the great Beast of Bas burn. They watched for as long as they could until the fire drove them away. A fallen tree came crashing down from high up in the burning mass, followed by a huge boulder that thundered towards them.

Neighing and frightened they turned and fled back across the valley. They crossed the small river and sheltered there as the fire burned on and on.

It burned for several more days.

Then Spit Fire and the Messenger took Heather and Olga home.

Once at their village, still keeping their distance from man-things, the unicorns left silently. The fire had enveloped the far reaches of the Forest of Eagla that stood on the foothills of the Mountains of Falling Stones. The smoke was clearly visible from the village and when Heather and Olga returned no questions were asked when they explained they'd foraged too far and their journey home cut off by the smouldering trees. But to go out again on their own they would find increasingly difficult; their parents would insist on a chaperone and at night the watch continued.

Several weeks passed and there was no news from the unicorns. The weather had turned colder and the first snows had fell.

The tribe was preparing for the coming cold; food preserved, meat dried, drinks fermented, wood dry stored for burning, everyone took part in these preparations. The long winter nights told stories round fires, wood carved into tools and art, linen spun and woven, clothes sewn with a fine bone needle, fur skins made into cloaks and boots. Soon it would be Solas-Tus, the festival to herald the coming of the light at the mid-winter solstice. They built pyres to be lit, prepared meat and tubers stuffed with nuts and dried berries, to be roast at the great feast. Gifts to give were made, music practised on drums and lyres, to be danced to all night. They dressed the sacred tree and chose the deer to be the gift, given to the god of gods at the height of their celebrations; the welcome of the dawn at the end of darkness at the end of the longest night.

But the time dragged for Heather as she lay awake wishing the unicorns would come. Worrying about whether they had traced the other unicorns now the fire had burnt out, whether the other two beasts had escaped or died in the fire too. She contemplated venturing out in the night, the darkness didn't encourage her and the colder weather brought the wolves and bears closer to their lands, but she was desperate to see them again. She made up her mind she would go. It was the night before the mid-winter solstice. Under the dim light of the embers of their cave fire she got up to gather some provisions to take, her mother was sleeping, and Olga too, her father out on watch. Then, when she looked up from a basket of nut bread, the room was getting steadily lighter. Spit Fire. It must be! She gently shook Olga, but she slept on, she skipped across the room and down to the wattle doorway. The golden light was streaming in now.

She pulled aside the door, the cold night air was crisp, and there was Spit Fire, standing all golden and majestic, though shaking from the exertion, his breath steaming from his nostrils. His thick mane now long enough to blow in the breeze, his muscles defined, and his horn almost full length, having grown quite some more since she last saw him. He was panting, he had galloped flat out all the way.

"We went to find the unicorns after the fire had subsided." Spit Fire began. "We went to look at the remains of the beast. There was no trace of the unicorns or Thoemanny or Dekserot. But the Beast of Bas... his bones were there, all bloody and raw. But breathing... we thought at first it was his body decomposing. We went back again and again to search the area for the unicorns. Each time his bones lay the same, slowly rising and falling... then I went again... earlier, and I saw his burnt charred bones slowly rise up out of the ashes, his one eye, intact, opened and looked at me, the other a hollow void. He creaked open his jaws and croaked an ear splitting roar that shook the ground. More bone than beast, I stood no longer and ran back to tell the others the terrible news. He is like a ghost. A Bas-Taibhse, a death-ghost...."

Heather gasped in horror.

Spit Fire continued, "If we go now we could track him, see where he goes, he must lead us to the other unicorns. It's our only hope."

Heather rushed back in to wake Olga and grab some food and furs. She hoped they wouldn't be gone longer than a night this time. Olga, bleary eyed, but now fully awake and keen for adventure, picked up her spear and Heather's axe.

They both climbed onto Spit Fire's back, now he was over three months older, he was stronger and broader, and could easily carry them both. With a whinny, mixed with fear and excitement, they took off into the moonlit night. Far off from the watch, they heard a shout, Spit Fire turned his head and looked back for an instant, just long enough for the watchers to pick out his golden horn, Heather and Olga looked back too, but their faces were indistinguishable, hidden in his mane. They carried on faster.

Faster and faster they went, it seemed that the land passed before them like a blur of shadows. Whoever had heard them back at their tribe would not be able to follow, and they hoped they had not been seen. Maybe they thought the whinny was from some of their own small dusky grey horses, or at least they hoped.

Spit Fire galloped on, and only slowed down as they approached the burnt out edges of the forest. It was quiet and eerie, no owl, bird or bat flew through the forest now. Picking his way through the charred tree stumps and ashes, they came to where the Beast of Bas-Taibhse had lain. The moon shone brightly and they could see that something large had made its passage through the dead trees; scored marks in the earth like one leg was dragged, and a distinctive heel and claw hollow, the shape of a paw without flesh. Following this they climbed cautiously upwards, higher up the mountain.

Once at the top they surveyed the land around, the Mountains of Falling Stones went on and on, capped with snowy peaks. It felt lonely and cold. They could not see Bas-Taibhse, but his track continued on across the mountain range and beyond. From the peak the going was easier, the slopes not so steep, just a sprinkling of snow over the dry land, strewn with large boulders and illuminated by the moonlight.

They continued to the edge of the mountain range, from there the beast's tracks led down into desert.

The first few rays of sunlight cast long shadows across the wide open desert sands. Turquoise and blue hues sculpted out peaks and valleys in the early light. Volcanoes lined the horizon, and between here and there the landscape was littered with holes, smoking and steaming. Heather and Olga had seen nothing like it.

There was no snow here, except for a fine dusty covering on a path that led through the land. It looked like Bas-Taibhse had followed this path, an occasional scurf and clawed print led them on, though they were getting fewer as the sand blew across and covered his tracks. As they walked on across the desert these tracks finally petered out. The desert undulated on for miles and miles all around and they had no idea which way the beast had gone.

They stopped. A deep crack cut across the path, like the land had split and opened, wide and long and dark. Spit Fire stood at its edge. Heather leaned forward and looked down into its depths, it was a thick black, smoke rising up made it difficult to see into it clearly, but she could make out small bits of red glowing and could feel heat rising up. Spit Fire wasn't looking in the great rift, his gaze followed the path to the horizon, where, midway between here and the volcanoes, stood four strange tall angular rocks. He sniffed the air, the smoke tainted his senses, but a thin scent of death and foreboding reached his nostrils. The hairs on his mane bristled. Absorbed with what lay ahead he lifted his hooves to carry on cautiously.

"Crack!" Heather had to shout, fearing he might step into the rift with her and Olga too. He turned about swishing his tail and prancing, as if he'd been having them on. Olga, now able to get a better view stared into the vast abyss.

"There's something moving down there!" Olga said.

They all turned round to look.

"Yes, I see it too," gasped Heather.

"I think it's molten lava," neighed Spit Fire.

Then the moving thing took shape and form and flew up out of the chasm. It landed beside them and they all took a step back and stared in awe as it spoke.

"You're a unicorn!" said the creature, and bowed. The creature was itself a small winged unicorn, the size of a young colt. "I thought I was the last." He arched his neck and fluttered his wings.

Spit Fire bowed too with the girls still on his back. "Spit Fire, your honour."

The winged unicorn stood up, with a short nod of his head, "Dark Fire. It is a great pleasure to meet you."

"And you," replied Spit Fire.

The winged unicorn, Dark Fire, was a storm cloud granite grey, with red glowing up his legs, from his hooves to his hocks. His mane and tail, longer than that of a colts, were a lighter grey fading to feldspar. His horn was a perfect spiral, crystal and golden. And his wings too, gold, sparkling and enchanting.

"How did you come to be here? Out in this desert? Alone?" asked Spit Fire.

Dark Fire spoke, "I've lived here alone in this fiery chasm all my life. It has given me life. Many years ago I was taken as a young foal by a great fire bird, rescued from the attack of the dragoss, flown far from home and dropped into this vast abyss. There I fell to my death. Yet, the fire bird had held me in its talons, and where it dug into my sides I grew wings, it gave me its strength and I lived. It told me I had five lives, though I have only two left. It told me my name is Dark Fire. A power over darkness. A power over fire. Both of which I have been learning and am yet to master. I am a fire unicorn."

Spit Fire bowed again. "Truly honoured to meet you. I have heard great stories of old of a foal taken by a fire bird, a special foal, inline to the King, the old King. But this was years ago and you are so young?"

"Time runs different here. A timeline, running through this rift. It is a beginning and an end, it is life and death. I am learning to master fire and for it to master me. But what brings you here? To this inhospitable land? I thought all the other unicorns were dead?" Dark Fire answered.

"No, we are a herd, though missing half. Half have been taken by three beasts; Thoemanny, Dekserot and Bas-Taibhse, the last, which we were tracking, brought us here, until we lost his tracks. He survived a great fire and now walks half bone, half ghost. His tracks led most of this way. We're hoping that he could lead us to the rest of our unicorns, if they are still alive... " Spit Fire's voice trailed off.

"The ogarths, dragoss and fire dogs... from the ancient times...." Dark Fire looked out over the horizon. "And what of the two man-things?"

"We're girls," said Heather and Olga flatly, in unison, now used to being referred to as man-things and having to correct whoever was addressing them.

"Man-things and unicorns? Man-things have hunted unicorns since before the ice!" Dark Fire neighed emphatically.

"They are helping us. They are my friends!" Spit Fire whinnied defensively.

Dark Fire looked into the girl's eyes, into their souls, studying them intently.

"Girls," whickered Dark Fire, deciding they could be trusted, "at your service." He bowed his proud head and glistening mane, then walked closer to them and let them touch his deep silken coat. Then looked directly at Spit Fire. "I would like to meet your King and your herd." Spit Fire turned his head and Dark Fire turned his and they nuzzled each other briefly in mutual understanding and unity.

Having lost the trail of the Beast of Bas-Taibhse and no sign or trace of the unicorns, they decided to return home. After all, the unicorns could have been taken somewhere else, or could have escaped, ...if they were alive still. There was no sign or trace of Thoemanny or Dekserot either. They would go home, for now and they left for the Valley of the Unicorns.

It had returned to night by the time they entered the valley. The stars lighting the way as Spit Fire led Dark Fire to meet the King. The Messenger stood looking on as they approached, the King and the elders at her side. They had been expecting them, the Messenger had sensed that something lost was returning, Dark Fire.

He was met with reverence, each unicorn bowed. The elders remembered when he was taken, many years ago when they were just foals, lost to the world and now returned. Dark Fire returned their bows and greeted them eagerly, glad to be home.

Heather and Olga, tired from their adventure, curled up in the long grass and fell asleep. Spit Fire nudged them with his nose, waking them, and set off to carry them swiftly to their home. As they left, Dark Fire and the unicorns exchanged stories of the years they'd lost, far into the night.

Spit Fire stayed at a distance so his tracks in the snow would not be obvious. All was quiet over at their caves. But through the trees, over the other side of the hill they could hear men walking through the undergrowth, and distant shouts. They walked through the bracken nearer to the noise to see what was going on. Ten or more tribesmen were holding blazing torches, spread out and tramping back towards their village, they sounded unsettled, tired and annoyed. Spit Fire re-traced his steps for fear of being seen. The girls dismounted, hugged him round his neck affectionately and ran lightly back across the clearing to their cave. They turned back, to see just a flash as Spit Fire disappeared. Heather looked up at the moon, it was still high in the sky, not far across its azimuth than when they left, they couldn't have been gone more than a few hours. The desert land, like Dark Fire said, must have a time of its own. They pushed open the door and crept inside, into their beds and under their covers of furs, unnoticed.

VII

THE TOWERS

The next morning it snowed heavily, falling like a silent blanket over the oaks, hazels and limes, covering any fresh tracks Spit Fire made last night. Heather and Olga slept very well. They awoke late to their mother stoking up the fire, the rich smell of freshly roasted hazelnuts, and sunlight streaming in through the doorway. They ventured outside, it had stopped snowing now and the land around sparkled with white, all glorious and pretty, a small robin came close and sat on a snow laden branch. They relaxed and threw snowballs, laughing and having fun, being children again, in anticipation of the coming evening's festivities for Solas-Tus, the winter solstice, at dawn.

Their father came in. He'd been drinking beer and talking with the elders straight from finishing his watch and not come in till now.

"We saw *unicorns* last night! Well I definitely saw one, and it had something on its back like an animal, and running away from our village!" Their father belched. He was tired, having been out all night searching for the unicorn and its quarry. "We didn't find it, it got too cold out there. But we are closer to knowing their routes and which direction they come from. We'll find them soon, they'll come closer in this cold, looking for food, just you watch. They're not going to take another child like from Yoster's tribe all those ages of the moon ago. Like we haven't got enough to worry 'bout, with a pack a wolves sighted too. Where's my bow? I'm going to get my arrows, fit those new arrow heads you got. Should have my own unicorn horn soon." He sat down heavily on his haunches beside the fire. The girls had come in after their father and heard his speech.

The eve of Solas-Tus was loud. Huge fires around the Trosban village lit the evening sky. Carved wooden shapes and clay figures were hung on an ancient yew, the everlasting green, the sacred tree; a deer, a dog, a basket of fruit, a woman heavy with child, each figure and shape representing their dreams and desires for the coming new year.

Olga placed her little clay unicorn secretly hidden within the branches and carved figures tied about the tree.

The tribes people drank and danced, and sang wild and soft melodies far into the night. By dawn it was a tired, relaxed and calm mood. They had gathered round their fire at Solas Aor watching the sun's first rays break through the herald stones, and fall upon the branches of the sacred tree. Olga sat with Heather, huddled under a large fur blanket made from several furs stitched together. She followed the sun's soft crisp light as it highlighted each of the shapes and figures on the tree, moving upwards through the branches. And there was her little unicorn, shining brightly, its polished pale clay catching the sun. As she and Heather walked back past the tree towards their home she retrieved her unicorn figure and tucked it away under the folds of her cloak. Keeping it safe, keeping it secret.

The next night Heather awoke to a bright intense golden light. She got up hurriedly, afraid for the unicorns after what she had learnt from her father. She woke Olga, their parents were sleeping soundly, tired and full from the Solas-Tus celebrations, remnants of the festival littered about their cave. Quietly both girls moved the wattle door aside.

Standing there outside was Spit Fire, Dark Fire and the King, glowing brightly and giving off a warmth that the girls could feel despite the cold and that melted the snow where they were standing. Dark Fire's coat and mane had started to go a darker shade of granite, the red on his legs fading. All three unicorns stood, powerful and elite, manes gently blowing in the night air, the moon slipping in and out of the clouds alternating highlights and shadows across their statures.

"We leave for the desert, we've just had news from the birds of the forest; they have reported seeing Dekserot and Thoemanny leaving with the unicorns across the desert just after the fire. You will come?" the King spoke first, the last sentence more an order than a request.

"Dark Fire has power over volcanoes!" neighed Spit Fire, impressively.

"I'm still learning to control it," said Dark Fire, with modesty.

Spit Fire interjected, "And with your help we have a better chance of finding the unicorns."

"And stop these beasts oppressing us and taking anymore of our herd," said the King.

The girls put on their felted tops and bound the loose culottes on their legs with leather. They grabbed their fur cloaks and left with the unicorns, Heather rode Spit Fire and Olga rode Dark Fire. Galloping across the night and the snow. They visited the unicorns' valley and there the King stayed, in charge over his herd.

Olga and Heather, Dark Fire and Spit Fire, set off over the mountains and into the desert. They followed the old snowy path, small flowers grew alongside, pretty, in emeralds, blues, violets and golds, and delicate, interlaced with the sand, stones and dust.

Dark Fire took the lead. The sun had risen and was high in the sky when they came to the great crack in the earth where Dark Fire had come from. They stopped and assessed the distance. It was no trouble for Dark Fire, he had wings to help him, but Spit Fire had to rely on the strength and power of his legs.

On Spit Fire's word Heather dismounted and climbed up onto Dark Fire's back behind Olga. Dark Fire gathered up his haunches and jumped easily, opening his wings once to steady his landing. For the girls it was an amazing feeling leaping the gap, they could feel the strength in Dark Fire's wings as he spread them wide.

Spit Fire trotted back a few strides and whinnied, calling across the gap to Dark Fire, who stood, looking back, whinnying encouragingly. He focussed on the other side, cleared his mind of all else around him and concentrated his whole body, judging the gap. In his mind he had already cleared it, knowing precisely how many steps until he jumped. With adrenalin tensing his muscles, like a coiled spring, he charged at the gap and leapt. He seemed frozen in time for a moment, midway over the chasm below, smoke and steam enveloping him, then his hooves smashed into the hard sand on the other side. His back legs scrambled to get a proper hold at the edge, but using the strength of his front legs, and with sheer will and power he got clear to stable ground. He was over.

The other side of the great chasm stretched out before them, more sculpted desert dotted with rocks and steaming holes. Heather picked a violet flower and got back onto Spit Fire, twisting it into his mane while they continued along the path, towards the four tall strange rocks looming in the distance.

The wind picked up, whipping up sand into writhing snakes across their path. Though there was no snow here, and the sun was hot, Heather and Olga were glad of their fur cloaks and wrapped legs. They rode on.

The tall rocks got ever closer.

They found themselves walking beneath their shadow, they were not rocks, they were towers. It felt cold, the towers casting an unnatural light. They had not seen anything like them before. They followed their hard angular edges with their eyes, looking up to their heights towering high above them. Each tower was different, yet all sculpted, hard, shiny and rock-like. One rose up like a column, a great smooth trunk, perfectly cylindrical, with larger cylindrical sections stacked up its height, but it was not made of wood. At its top sat a dome, smooth like the top of a bald man's skull. The other three towers were angular, one soared high with a spike on its top. Another had sides of unequal lengths, smooth and straight, the top forming a sharp angle. The last one was similar but shorter. Despite their unnatural shape and structure they looked old, worn and broken. As Olga studied them she could see thin cracks all the way up their sides.

"These are not made by nature alone. They must have been made by hands, great hands, giant hands. Do you know who built them?" asked Spit Fire to Dark Fire.

"I don't know," replied Dark Fire. "I never noticed them

before, when I was first brought here by the fire bird. The volcanoes were more active then, and the land was thick with smoke, I wouldn't have seen far. I don't know. I sense an ill feeling, I can't explain it. My horn aches, there is a kind of power here."

They continued walking around the towers. They found nothing and the desert stretched out away from them for miles and miles. The wind had blown sand and covered any tracks of beasts or unicorns.

Heather looked up and noticed a flame flashing at the top of the trunk-like tower. "Look!" she gasped and they all stared.

"I'll take a closer look," whinnied Dark Fire. "I'll fly up and look around. Do you want to fly Olga?"

Dark Fire gathered his wings and, not waiting for Olga to decline, within a few beats he was up flying high towards the flashing flame. Olga gripped Dark Fire's glossy mane and held on tightly. This was such a thrill, to soar up high, be spun around as he changed direction, to feel weightless and excited. Once air borne the view was tremendous, on and on, to the distant volcanoes and back the other way, to the great chasm, the narrow path winding across the sand and she could just make out the Mountains of Falling Stones.

The dome was all smooth, the flame underneath, contained in a type of ice, twinkling, unexplainably. The tower didn't give much away from the outside, was there a way in? Dark Fire plunged back down to the others, Olga felt her stomach lurch and she gasped as she was taken by surprise by their quick decent.

Back on the ground, the girls dismounted, they sat in the shade and ate some sweet nut-breads they'd brought with them. Olga, leaning her back against a tower, noticed a thin crack that formed a regular line going up from where she sat to twice the height of her, then across above her head, twice as far again, and then back down. Tracing her fingers along its line she called out to the others. Both girls placed their palms either side of the vertical cracks and pushed against it. It moved inwards....

The air seemed to be drawn in through the doorway that they had pushed open. Hairs on the back of their necks bristled, Olga stepped in first, and she was inside the huge column tower. A vast circular space, dark and cold. In the centre was a large puddle of what looked like water, dark and inky. Long vertical blocks that rose up against the far wall formed steps spiralling up and disappearing into the darkness. And it was so quiet. In some way the girls found that reassuring, and curiosity egged them on. Along the steps there were markings cut deep into the wall. Strange lines and shapes that they did not recognise. Olga touched them with her finger tips, intrigued, as she took a step upon the blocks. The steps were wide enough for the unicorns to walk side by side, and they and Heather stepped past Olga, who was still touching the strange hieroglyphics, and went on upwards.

As they continued up the steps a red glow came from ahead, which got steadily brighter the nearer they got to its source. It must be from the flame that burned at the top of the tower.

Olga was following some way behind them, her eyes now accustomed to the darkness, the hieroglyphics continued all the way up the wall, her fingers continued to trace their sharp lines. She looked back the way she had come and exclaimed... there, lying beneath the inky puddle, and only now visible from this height, was an image of the three beasts, each entwined with one another, stylised and twisted, in combat. The Beast of Thoemanny stood square and tall in the middle between the two. The others came back down to see why she'd shouted out and what she was looking at. They all stood still. The red light seemed to be getting stronger. They all felt more and more uneasy. Not yet making any sense of it Dark Fire turned and continued back up the steps to see what was at the top, Heather and Spit Fire followed, Olga, slowly and more cautiously took up behind. She turned to look back again at the image of the beasts under the shallow dark covering of water. It was strangely bewitching. She stood still, transfixed. The water rippled, she was sure she could make out her own image reflected in the water, and, what was that? The image of the third beast.... She was sure it moved! She took a step backwards and put out her arms to steady herself, expecting to feel the cold rock wall. She gasped. She had put her hand on warm bone!

It happened very fast, a giant clawed paw grabbed her in its bony grasp... she cried out, but it took her back down the steps and out into the light and the desert. The Beast of Bas-Taibhse!

Dark Fire, Spit Fire and Heather heard Olga's cries and all came tripping and half falling down the steps and out of the tower. They saw her struggling in the giant beast's skeletal-like paw, as the beast dragged its body across the sands. Heather jumped up onto Spit Fire's back and Dark Fire took off into the air after the beast. Spit Fire charging after it as it ran awkwardly, still trailing its back leg behind. Despite its injuries it was moving fast. Spit Fire could only just keep up.

Dark Fire kept diving down to catch it and get it to release Olga, but the beast's thick skin was unflinching to his attacks. It turned its great bony head, baring its teeth, snarling and snapping at Dark Fire.

And the beast ran on and on, covering the rocky desert with vast strides, towards the volcanoes.

Dark Fire flying fast flew off ahead of the beast, until he

reached the first volcano, there he hovered above its smoking crater, beating his wings. He neighed and whinnied and pointed his horn into its core. Again and again he tried, commanding it, willing it, straining to control the power he possessed, concentrating his energy to his horn as he beat his wings, streams of smoke billowing up through his mane.

Heather looked on from Spit Fire's back, in awe, she saw what looked like lightning connecting from his horn to the volcano, and she felt and heard the volcano rumble. Then there was a loud crack and the volcano burst, splitting its sides and belching hot ash into the sky. Engulfed in the ash Dark Fire suddenly fell, plummeting down into the widening crater, she saw it swallowing him up and he was gone. She looked on in horror.

"No! Dark Fire!" she cried.

The volcano rumbled and lava came flooding down towards the beast and Olga. Bas-Taibhse held Olga in his tight, solid grip. Petrified but unharmed, her attempts at squirming free were futile.

Spit Fire ran on, it was down to him now. He was on his own. Distraught and stupefied by what he'd seen, he summoned up his energy and focused on saving Olga, trying to get near as the beast swung down his forearm that carried Olga, hoping to catch her if she got free. He ran on and on.

Then, there was a cry, a neigh!

And Dark Fire burst up through the cloud of ash. He neighed to the volcano and flew out of the clouds towards the beast. He joined Spit Fire and Heather, and they both drove the beast on towards the rolling lava and ash surrounding them.

Dark Fire encircled the beast, trying to get him to free Olga, he flew round and round, it was now or never, the lava was a step away, Bas-Taibhse, trying to steady himself, released his grip around Olga and threw her away, up in the air and roared an almighty throaty roar. Dark Fire swooped right down at that moment and caught her in mid flight, just before she hit the ground. Spit Fire reared up and turned away, Heather, clinging onto his back, tears streaming down her face, relieved Dark Fire was alive and Olga was safely on Dark Fire's back. And they ran and flew in the other direction as fast as they could, running for their lives, as the lava and ash cloud spread out over the desert. Dark Fire stalling in the sky to take one last look back at the Beast of Bas-Taibhse as the lava enveloped him and he sank groaning beneath its curtain of ash to his death.

Sometime later they cantered back up the hill to Heather and Olga's home. It had turned night again as they left the desert, and now, once back again in their home, the clouds continued to flit across the moon as they had the night they left. Heather and Olga were unsure if they'd been gone a whole night or if this was the same night when they had left. They climbed down off the unicorns' backs and threw their arms around their necks and hugged them. Heather put her forehead against Spit Fire's muzzle, they needed no words. Both girls and unicorns stood like that, solemnly in solace, for a while. Dark Fire was the first to speak.

"We may not come again for a while, let the snows pass. Thoemanny's injured, Dekserot's far away, Bas-Taibhse is dead. The volcano will have destroyed much of the towers and the desert land. The taken unicorns are lost...." Dark Fire's big eyes, deep, thoughtful and sorrowful, looked from both girls and then out into the distance.

"What happened out there? You fell? We thought you had died," Heather asked Dark Fire.

"I did," he replied. "The ash cloud sank into my lungs and burnt, I was overcome and fell to my death. My fourth life spent."

Both girls and Spit Fire looked at him astonished. "So, by five lives, you actually die five times?" Heather's jaw dropped.

"Yes, it's not pleasant," he whinnied, nibbling an itch on his side. "We must leave you now." And both unicorns lifted up their heads in parting. "Farewell, till next time."

"Farewell," the girls called after them. They stood and watched the unicorns canter off into the night. When they could see them no more they turned to go back to their cave.

The wattle door was just as they'd left it, just partially wedged, enough to secure their home but still able to open. Their mother lay sleeping soundly, their father next to her, snoring like a boar. It looked like they had only been gone three or four hours. They climbed into their beds of furs, stony cold from being empty. Olga gathered up her bedding, even the woven matting stuffed with bracken that formed her mattress and her clay unicorn that she'd hidden under her pillow. She put the gathered bundle down next to Heather and lay it all out. Both sisters cuddled up together, for warmth and security, and pulled their covers close around them.

VIII

THOEMANNY

It snowed the next day and for another two weeks, gently covering the tracks the unicorns had left. But not soon enough.

Early the next morning Greyla the elder had been out tracking boar with her dog, looking for truffles under the hazels and oaks. She'd gathered a small handful, neatly stowed away in her deerskin bag, when she came across Dark Fire's and Spit Fire's hoof marks. These were much larger marks than their own small sturdy horses they kept close by. She bent over them. Her old withered frame not able to straighten, she leant her weight on her staff and examined the area and ground around them, she noted the direction they came from and where they went. She noticed the fading yellow gold dust that speckled the frozen snow. She noticed a flaxen golden hair, long, silky yet coarse, unmistakably equine. She noticed the footmarks of two of her own kind, making their way towards the watchers' caves... the snow had melted nearer to the caves, the direction the trails took, less evident, but she had her suspicions....

Over the weeks snow turned to rain, making the frozen ground thaw and turn red from the sandy earth. A snowdrop sprung its head up above ground, one of the first flowers of early spring, and an early wood anemone cautioned a bud, the winter had seemed eternal to the two sisters and there had been no more contact from the unicorns.

Greyla had returned from her foraging for truffles, and gone straight to hold council. Stirring up the threat from unicorns as an increasing urgency. Then, one of their horses had disappeared, silently, at night, right under the watchers' glare, it didn't look like a lone wolf ...and the wolf pack had been successfully driven away a full cycle of the moon ago. Then deer disappeared, one by one, every few weeks. Strange large animal tracks found in the mud and scars on tree trunks that resembled marks left by a horn, possibly a unicorn horn....That creature they'd seen on the unicorn's back, was it beast? Or was it of their own tribe? Councils had met again, and again, barley whisky drunk in quantity, the ritual horn passed around and smoked, trances sustained, insight reached and accusations pointed. Heather and Olga felt the eyes looking sideways at them, suspicions and rumours running rife, their father being a watcher as well. The Trosban tribe was uneasy.

But Greyla wasn't the only one who had seen the unicorns' tracks....

Heather stirred the embers of the fire, daydreaming about

Spit Fire and the unicorns, it had been a very long time now since they last saw them. The fire spat, sending a spark scurrying across the floor, it reminded her of the night she sat with the Messenger and her new born foal and thought up his name. She reached under Olga's pillow of furs and retrieved the little clay unicorn that was kept tucked away there, turning it round in her hands, tracing the shape of it with her fingers. That night she went to sleep a little uneasy and yet a little excited with a sense of something about to happen. It was almost dawn when there came the familiar yellow glow. Heather woke easily and she found Olga was already awake. Both sisters, keen to see the unicorns again, to reassure their friendship and dispel the doubts created by the villagers' rumours, eagerly crept to the doorway, and as quietly as they could, moved aside the wattle. The glow was there, filling the clearing in front of their cave, coming from down the bank, but no unicorns. They must be standing in the trees, perhaps to avoid being seen.

Heather called out quietly, "Spit Fire, Dark Fire."

They walked across the clearing and towards the trees and undergrowth where the golden glow was intensified, stepping over the new ferns and new growth of spring, stepping through the trees going down the hill. Then they heard a branch crack to their left, they looked left, expecting to see their familiar friends, but there behind a young oak some horns moved... two horns, two upwardly curving horns, attached to a head as one, like that of a bull, two sullen eyes looked back.... Olga stepped back and reached for Heather's hand, neither dared utter a word. Thoemanny....

The beast rose up slowly out of the undergrowth where he'd been squatting, straightened himself to his full height and stood staring out at them. Heather and Olga froze. He was too close for them to both run back past him to their cave, and their cave was that bit just too far to outrun him. The two sisters remained frozen. The cold morning air gave his breath a foggy shape, he sniffed, he looked old, his tired lonely eyes continued to stare at them. He moved forward, slow and unsteady on his hind legs, Heather and Olga shifted close to each other, terrified. Two unicorn horns and a dead capercaillie swung from a hide thong around his middle, a guttural noise came from deep within his throat, he seemed to be saying something of importance to them. Both girls took a step back, on the brink of making a run for it, stepping into one another, Heather fell on top of Olga. Olga's foot, treading into soft earth, slid under a tree root, and with Heather's weight on top, got wedged fast. Thoemanny, now standing in front of the oak, bent, steadying himself placing his clawed dark hand on his left thigh, and breathed a low hollowing growl. Both girls scrambled to get up; Olga twisted and pulled at her leg, Heather pulling her sister's arm not realizing she was stuck. Olga struggled, her hands went down to her foot, digging hurriedly in the earth. Though the first few inches of earth were soft, below her foot was rock. Heather panicking started throwing anything she could find at the beast.

Facing the frightened girls and unflinching at the assault of flying logs, leaves and stones, Thoemanny lunged another two strides forward, he bent down, his bones creaking, he was bending over both girls.

Both girls closed their eyes and cried out.

He grabbed Olga's defending arm and held it up, holding it fast. He reached down to the wet root trapping her foot, closed his large clawed hand around it and tore it out of the earth. All in the same movement he released her arm that he held tight and stood up, his great hulk swaying with the action of tearing out the root which he now held above his head. He stood there. A kind of distant sadness came over his eyes. He uttered the same guttural tones again and coughed.

Heather and Olga hurriedly stood up, pausing briefly, bewildered.

Thoemanny, grunted and growled a mumble. His eyes looked wet. He threw the root aside, holding his gaze upon the girls for a moment longer.... And then he left. As he retreated back into the thick of the bushes, he noticed a tall figure hurrying across the bank, long hair falling loose behind, feet bare, legs slender like a deer, it was another female.

Heather and Olga scrambled back up the bank and into their cave, pulses racing, sweating and white, they pushed fast the wattle door and jammed the log against it. Shivering they hugged each other. Their cave was empty. They knew their father was out on watch tonight, but where was their mother? Fear rushed up into their throats like a sickening weight, suddenly fearful for her safety they ran back outside calling, "Mother! Mother!"

She wasn't far, she came running to their calls, she gathered them in her arms, hugging them tight in her comforting reassuring embrace. She had awoken from their cries and finding their beds empty had run off in search of them, though she had run in the opposite direction to where they had been.

Back at their cave, the girls relayed their story of how Olga had got her foot stuck under a root, but omitted the part about the beast. They desperately wanted to tell their mother everything but were scared that if they told her about the beasts, they would have to tell her about the unicorns, and the Glowing Caves, and then she would tell their father. Their father, being a watcher, was bound by tribal law to relay all information to the elders. With the disappearances of the tribe's horses and deer, with unicorn tracks found and unicorn sightings, and with some 'creature' on its back, the Trosban tribal elders were convinced unicorns and some 'beast' were working together, the evidence so convincing that even Heather and Olga, even after all their adventures with the unicorns, had started to wonder if it could be true. And now Thoemanny coming to their cave? Yet unicorn horns were very valuable and in high demand, to cure ills and to protect the tribe. If the elders knew where the Unicorn Valley was they would lead the hunters to hunt the last of them, put a stop to their threat and take their horns. Despite their shadow of doubt growing in their minds, Heather and Olga kept their secret.

The next night Heather awoke to the golden glow again, she woke Olga fervently, checking their mother was still sleeping, they crept down towards the doorway. There they waited. And listened. They could hear nothing. Heather moved the fur hanging over the wattle door aside, and put her eyes close up to the cracks in the woven hazel, still nothing, she couldn't see far enough. The sisters looked at one another. If they could just shift one edge of the door a bit back without opening it, it could allow them to see through. Carefully they pulled at the one edge, peering into the small crack of an opening, Olga now pushing her face right up close, suddenly there was a snort of hot air right back at her and she fell backwards. Heather looked at her with alarm but, Olga's face quickly turned to laughter and she got up to pull the door fully open. There, up close and peering down at them both was Dark Fire, still snorting with dust up his nose and Spit Fire standing behind him. With such relief the girls threw their arms around the unicorns and buried their faces in their soft coats. Friends had returned, doubts dispelled.

Dark Fire had grown, standing, muscles toned and

twitching, his coat now completely black, glossy and fine, his golden wings larger and more powerful. Spit Fire, next to him, matched him in muscle and height, with a strong dark golden coat and glistening mane. Collecting a few things to take and closing the door behind them the sisters got on the unicorns' backs and were soon trotting under the cover of the trees, retelling their horror of the previous night and Thoemanny's uncharacteristic behaviour.

Dark Fire whinnied, "I wouldn't trust him. The way he worked with Dekserot, like he'd trained him, had him under his control. So this means they both could still be close, have there been any sightings of either beast?"

Heather replied, "No, I don't think so, though some strange tracks were found that could have been them. They found your tracks, they think you're...." She paused, that nagging doubt stalling her, no, the unicorns couldn't be working with the beasts? She continued, changing the subject, "The watchers are out every night."

Dark Fire, turned his handsome head towards Heather as they slowed to a walk, walking side by side. "We're going to go and explore the land beyond the volcanoes."

Olga darted a glance at Heather, half fear, half excitement, then turned back securing her grip on Dark Fire's mane. The first light of dawn filtered through the edge of the trees and they set off.

Breaking out of the woods and picking up speed, they found themselves galloping fast over hills and streams, through the Glowing Caves and across the Unicorn Valley and making their passage through the Mountains of Falling Stones, to the desert, to adventure.

Thoemanny sat at the entrance to the cave lion's cave and

threw a small piece of fresh deer rump at the lion. It ate
hungrily. It had been unable to hunt since it had caught its leg
in Thoemanny's trap and torn it badly. The beast had been
feeding it this way for some days, gaining its trust. The rest of
the deer rump lay at his feet, now he took out a living stone
from a pouch slung round his middle, and played with it in his
hand. Passing it from hand to hand, watching the lion closely,
watching the lion watching him, watching him play with the
living stone in front of the deer rump. The lion's mouth
drooled, it snarled, it was still very hungry. Thoemanny
continued to pass the living stone from hand to hand, it shone
and spun, a mind of its own, it jumped up and hovered for a
moment in mid-air, then back into Thoemanny's hands. It was
hypnotising the lion. Thoemanny was well accustomed to these
living stones and he used them with skill. He thought it was
time now to try something new. A challenge, a test. All animals
respected unicorns, they held them in awe, the protectors of the
forest, they would never harm one.

Thoemanny took out a new piece of meat, he sliced it with
his claw, then threw the newly carved chunk of unicorn flesh,
at the lion.... It snarled, sniffed, then lowered its head, and ate...
The training was begun. This cave lion would be useful to help
him hunt.

Crossing the desert Heather and Olga, Dark Fire and Spit
Fire, came to the smoking ashen lava field left by the volcano
when it erupted. The sculpted lava had set hard and black, parts
covered with thick layers of grey ash, smoke drifting out of
cracks. The towers still stood. Though one was almost engulfed
by lava, and ash painted them all a dull grey. They didn't stop.
Walking on they came across the remains of Bas-Taibhse, half
buried in the lava, frozen there in his struggle, completely skull

and bones. Carrion birds still picking at his ribs, it was a grotesque image.

"Stop, please," said Olga. She dismounted and walked closer to study the great clawed paw that had once held her in terror back at the beginning of winter. Stooping over it she bent down and tentatively lifted one of its large claws. It broke off in her hand. Studying it for a moment, the size of it the length of her arm, she put it in her soft deerskin bag that was slung across her shoulder and climbed back up on Dark Fire's back. They carried on along their journey, carefully picking their way across the lava field and beyond.

Beyond, the land changed, it became more fertile, lush grasslands that rolled down for miles, small trees sprung up here and there and starred with many bright flowers. On the horizon they could see a silver shimmering, the sea.

IX

THE SEA

The sun had now risen high in the sky and beat down with a fierceness on the hot sand as the four travellers touched the sand dunes. Picking their way down through the soft dunes, the sand levelled out to a wide flat expanse. Dark Fire and Spit Fire, nostrils flared, catching the sea air, felt the thrill of the wide open space. The sea beckoned them forward as they spelt out their marks across the beach and raced to the sea.

Jumping and splashing through the breaking waves, the unicorns played, the girls laughing at getting drenched, it was cool and refreshing in the hot sun. They slid off the unicorns' backs, splashing each other and the unicorns, and waded back to the beach, Heather opening her deerskin bag to see if the contents of sweet-bread and dried fish had not got soggy. The ones at the bottom had, and she broke off the ruined pieces and threw them out to the seabirds and crabs. Pulling out the rest and sharing them with Olga, to eat them before they also got ruined by the sodden bag, they walked up to some rock pools and sat down taking in the peaceful view. The sea was like a majestic body, deep blue and turquoise, the sun glistening on its surface as the waves gently rolled along the beach. Both sea and beach went on for miles, it was so calm, so hot and so relaxing, almost hypnotising staring out to sea. A place far away from beasts and tribal troubles, a place to be absorbed and immersed in the scene. Behind them, the dunes rose up becoming high cliffs and further on, out to sea, they could make out an island, green and mountainous.

"Let's explore!" announced Olga. Heather took her eyes away from the view, Spit Fire and Dark Fire had walked back up to the grassy plains and were munching tranquilly on the rich grass.

"Yes, alright, up on those cliffs?" Heather replied. And the sisters, leaving their bags and cloaks drying on the rocks, having squeezed out the water from the bottom of their tunics, allowing them to dry as they walked, set off towards the cliffs.

A breeze had picked up as they walked along the cliff top, fanning them and filling them with energy. They had walked quite a way, as they looked back towards the unicorns, who were just small figures in the landscape, and grey heavy clouds had massed inland, hanging over them.

"We should get back," said Olga, but then spotted a cave in the cliffside below them. "But shall we just take a look in there?"

Heather and Olga took the small path leading down the cliff to the large cave opening and they ventured inside. Where it was sheltered from the wind and elements, hoofmarks and large unusual prints littered the soft sandy earth of the cave floor.

"Look!" both girls exclaimed together, then immediately were quiet, thinking that the larger marks could be of the beasts.

"Let's get Spit Fire and Dark Fire," said Heather quietly, and with light steps they ran out of the cave and back up the path, then ran full speed across the cliff top and over the grassy plains towards the unicorns.

"Dark Fire, Spit Fire!" they called out, catching their breath. "We've found hoof prints and beasts' prints too possibly, we should check it out."

Dark Fire and Spit Fire trotted over and stood still for the girls to mount them, then broke into a fast canter until they reached the cliffside path. Carefully walking down the path they entered the cave. All was quiet, just the muffled sound of the breeze outside and the sea crashing on the base of the cliff below as the tide was coming in. Spit Fire lowered his head and sniffed the marks. Dark Fire did the same.

"Unicorns, old marks, but unicorns," Spit Fire snorted, nostrils twitching, eyes roamed around the cave.

Dark Fire was sniffing the other marks. "Dekserot," he nickered. "Unmistakably." He continued walking around the cave floor, examining the other traces. "Thoemanny too. Though looks like these were left before the winter. They lead down that tunnel." And he started off, down the tunnel following the trail of prints. Spit Fire and the girls followed him, all on foot. The tunnel led down and down. The tunnel walls were decorated with strange long lines and circular marks, they seemed to depict a story, a message? A warning? Similar hieroglyphics to those in the tall towers. Olga remembered tracing their lines and shapes before, she felt uneasy. The girls walked behind the unicorns, they only walked a short way, it was so dark, there was no glow like in the

Glowing Caves.

"We need some light," Dark Fire neighed, turning his head around, "this tunnel goes on quite a way, and it's pitch black." Then addressing Heather and Olga. "Can you make fire? I think I can help, find something to hold a flame."

They walked back towards the cave opening. Looking around the cave floor and then outside for some wood and kindling. Heather broke off a branch from a shrub growing on the cliff top, at one end it split it into three branches and into this frame she pushed some dry grass and dry moss making a nest of it and then wrapping it in tightly twisted grasses. She found a small amount of hardened tree sap and pushed this into the top of the grass and moss. She hoped her rough fashioned torch would do. They had no bullrushes here which keep their flame slow and long. She set about looking for two sticks to rub together and create friction and smoke.

Dark Fire interrupted her search. "That's good. Hold it out at arms length, in front of me. I'm going to try something."

He arched his powerful neck and bent his head, directing his horn towards the torch in Heather's outstretched hand. Olga and Spit Fire watched on. Dark Fire concentrated, his eyes rolled and closed, out of his horn came a thin lilac light, when it reached the torch it became an intense purple and then the torch smoked, glowed and a small flame took light. He opened his eyes and shook his long black mane with a snort of pleasure.

They set off quickly down the tunnel, the torch would not burn too long, but they hoped it would give them chance to investigate where these prints led. The tunnel led downhill, wide enough for the four of them to walk side by side. As they went deeper down the muffled sound of the sea got louder, and at the next twist in the tunnel they stepped into ankle deep water. The water seemed to ripple and surge like waves, they must be near the sea and this water could be the tide coming in. As they listened carefully, above the sound of the water came a low sizzling and hissing sound.

They cautiously went a bit further, the tunnel led up again, out of the water. It grew wider and its roof higher, opening out into a chamber. Long thin turquoise stalactites hung down intertwined with twisted helictites at crazy angles. The glow from the dying torch reflecting amber sparkles of dancing crystals in the formations. The four wandered through the vaulted chamber marvelling at nature's cave sculptures. A balcony ledge led up from the floor along the length of the chamber and on through to a vast gallery. This seemed to be the end of the tunnel, at its centre, some way down, lay a large pool of water. The wide ledge led around the pool, the sides were filled with elegant emerald like stalagmites, some shooting up from the mirrored surface of the water and the same crystalline walls all around. The last of their torchlight was reflected in the green shards, which bounced and shone from shard to shard around the gallery; creating tall shadows and shapes of light that played on the surface of the pool below.

The sizzling sound had got louder and was now accompanied by a low bubbling. Suddenly a blast of steam shot up from the rock beneath them, just in front of Dark Fire and Olga who were leading, making them all jump and Olga slid off Dark Fire's back.

"This is volcanic land, a dormant volcano and these are active hot springs. I have heard of places like this," Dark Fire breathed. "It feels my presence, I think this is why it's waking up."

"It's waking up?" said Olga, alarmed, "But you can stop it

yes? Being master of fire and all?"

"I think I have the opposite effect... unfortunately in this case," Dark Fire replied.

Heather got off Spit Fire to join Olga on foot, who was now looking at the crystal formations in detail, steam trickled out of cracks in the rock walls and the air got hotter, the rock walls felt warm. Since they had met the water in the tunnel, the unicorn hoof prints had gone, possibly washed away by the rising tide. They walked along the balcony ledge around the crystalline gallery. The pool lay below to one side, its walls heavily encrusted with crystals of greens, turquoise and emerald; some lay scattered on the rock floor, and some stalagmites fallen like something large had passed through and knocked them.

Just then they heard a faint tink, a trickle of a noise, Dark Fire whinnied unnervingly. It seemed to come from a pile of fallen crystals, one of which shone brightly, a crystal sphere, solid fiery gold in its heart with a silver halo shimmering around it. Both girls were drawn towards it, it was beautiful and shiny. Then came the noise again. It rolled off the pile and came to a stop at Olga's feet. She bent down and lifted it in her hand, Heather looking on. They exclaimed! In her hand it came alive... a living rock! It writhed and twisted and pulled her hand, containing some force that could not be seen.

"Drop it, it's a living stone!" neighed Dark Fire. "They have an ancient power, from a time before. They are a free spirit, unpredictable and dangerous."

But it was already tugging her. She still held it in her hand, unable to resist its strange magnetic power. And before the unicorns or Heather could act Olga was pulled by its force over the balcony and into the depths of the pool below....

Underwater she was pulled down, she was unable to loosen

her grip. She heard Heather and the unicorns jump in after her, but it was pulling her down fast. There was a light, the stone took her towards this light and past it, back up and she was out of the water, inside the very heart of the dormant volcano. There she heard a thundering cry, a roar, echoing round the old hollow crater. And then came neighs, and the sound of hooves stamping on rock. She wiped the water from her eyes with her free hand and there she saw them... the unicorns, and standing guard, a beast, solid, black and with two great tails....

Dark Fire reared up out of the water, shaking and stretching his wings, using them to spring out of the water and stand at the side of the pool, a streak of fear in the whites of his eyes. Spit Fire, with Heather holding on swimming at his side, climbed up and out onto the edge of the pool alongside Olga. The sleepy volcano belched, a shot of steam blasted upwards. A narrow shaft of light broke through the vaulted roof of the crater and lit the floor below. Streaks of many colours blazoned up the rock walls, grass and moss grew on the buttress slopes and there standing together in the centre of the crater were the lost unicorns, twenty or more of them, terrified eyes of forgotten hope staring back at them. Pegasus, the King of the Sky was there too, and two more winged horses, and the old king unicorn that Dark Fire recognised from before he was taken. It was a solid prison, no way out except through the pool, the thin shafts of light through the roof were not large enough for a winged horse or unicorn to fly through. And the Beast of Dekserot guarded the pool.

The beast stood there facing Dark Fire. His two great tails thrashing from side to side. He roared again, lifting his head and giving a great cracking croak.

Dark Fire reared up again and neighed to the depths of the unsettled volcano, he needed it to rouse, to distract the beast, to help him free the unicorns. The volcano slumbered on. Again he neighed, he flew up beating his wings, and dived back down, from the belly of the earth beneath them came a slow laboured rumble. Then a blast of hot air shot upwards beside Dekserot sending a huge rock up into the great crater's chimney. Dekserot unbalanced.

Dark Fire screamed a neigh at the unicorns to come forward. Steam and smoke filled the crater. Dark Fire flew around the beast, dodging his tails as the crater shot more rocks and steam up into the air.

Dekserot opened his jaws and hissed a fiery roar of hot air and flames, spilling across the floor like liquid.

Dark Fire twisted and jumped using his wings to gain height and using his newly harnessed power to force the beast's flames back, screaming again at the unicorns to run.

The unicorns and winged horses, terrified and weak from their imprisonment, saw their way through the flames and charged towards the pool.

The stone was shining brightly in Olga's hand, blindingly. It got intensely hot, then suddenly went frozen like a solid lump of ice and Olga, sitting on the edge of the pool, dropped it; its magnetic force locking her fingers around it disintegrated. It rolled, now dull and lifeless. Heather bent down and picked it up. She took Olga's arm and both girls climbed on Spit Fire's back, took a deep breath and plunged under the water. Following the light shining through the water they found themselves surfacing in the sea at the base of the cliffs. Other unicorns burst through the water beside them, five, six, seven, more, then the old King, then Pegasus and the winged horses. They trod water, waiting desperately for Dark Fire to emerge. The top of the cliff was now bellowing a steady smoke and steam, and the sleepy rumbling had become a constant groan.

Unicorns were striking out to shore, Pegasus and those that had wings were flying high above, all making a mass exodus to the distant beach. Spit Fire and the girls stayed in the water, anxious, waiting for Dark Fire, it had been a long time now. Then the waters went quiet, the grumbling volcano resumed a low rumble, unusually quiet, like it was waiting to erupt spectacularly. Then, just as Spit Fire was going to plunge back under water to go back for Dark Fire, Dark Fire broke out of the water, bursting into the sky with his powerful wings, soaring up high. In mid flight he stalled and shook his wet mane, neighed a farewell and gratification to the volcano and called to Spit Fire and the girls to make for shore.

Standing on the shore Heather looked down at her palm, she opened it and there lay the living stone that she'd held tightly in her clutch. On releasing her grip the stone flinched a couple of times, then, suddenly, became alive and jumped up and into the sea. Heather, still unsure about the stone but drawn to it, found herself diving after it. She reached into the surging water and grabbed it. It pulled her down, down and under the waves, into blackness.

She found herself back in the cave with the emerald stalagmites; sitting on the pool's edge, her feet in the water, stunned and bewitched by the stone. The cave was dark and empty, a faint glow from the stone echoed around the shards of stalagmites, but she didn't feel alone. She stared around the cave as if she was just waking up from a dream, she felt a presence. Abruptly, close to her face, a pair of yellow eyes opened and a hollow voice came from the darkness....

"Follow the eyes, Heather...."

Other voices echoed around her.

"No! Throw the stone at the eyes! Run before it's too late!"

They were hypnotising, far and distant.

"Don't listen to them! Listen to me, give the stone to the eyes and sleep here till morning...."

It was intense, the voices, invading her mind, a fog bearing down in her head. She couldn't bare it.

"No!" she screamed and threw the stone wildly away from her falling backwards into the black inky water and unconsciousness.

Opening her eyes she could make out light filtering under the rocks from the sky above the sea, and she saw three shapes moving towards her through the water.

Spit Fire, Dark Fire and Olga were swimming towards her, looking for her, with relief they found her and helped her swim to shore.

"Those living stones are dangerous! I told you!" scolded Dark Fire. "What happened down there?"

Heather was pale. "There were three sets of eyes in the darkness. The stone pulled me to the cave with the emerald stalagmites. And there were voices coming from the eyes, ...telling me to go with them!" She shuddered.

"The ancient spirits. The dark spirits." Dark Fire looked back towards the sea. "They wouldn't come out when I was there. I have a kind of power over darkness and the spirits within it and they fear me."

"They could have claimed your soul! Then you would have been lost to this world forever!" neighed Spit Fire alarmingly.

Dark Fire continued, "It was the cave where you found the stone?"

"Yes, but I threw it away," replied Heather, tears running down her cheeks. She rubbed her face and hugged her arms around herself. Dark Fire bent his head down to her and nuzzled her shoulder comfortingly.

"It's alright," he neighed, then, addressing all the unicorns and winged horses now gathered on the beach. "The Beast of Dekserot has been injured by the flying rocks inside the crater. I don't know how long he will lie there, I had to leave, as the crater is unstable. He could rise again, so we must all retreat to our valley and gather our strength and prepare to protect our herd and fight. The Beast of Thoemanny is still roaming the lands. We must make haste."

The volcano had remained quiet, just an occasional rumble, the thick smoking turret had ebbed, it wasn't happy at being woken and it slept on, for now.

Dark Fire and Spit Fire cantered across the beach leading all the unicorns and winged horses, Heather and Olga riding on their backs, stopping only to gather their cloaks and bags. Here, in this time-locked land, the sun was setting over the sea, sending streaks of pinks and crimson across the sky and pink dancing surf on the waves. Thin trails of smoke from the cliff, tinged with a fiery crimson and purple, joined the sunset clouds as the liberated unicorns and winged horses began their journey home.

X

SOLAS~TAIU

At the Trosban village Heather and Olga's mother was swimming in the clear waters of the pools at the bottom of the hill. It was early morning, washed and refreshed, she got out of the tranquil waters to dress. As she wrung out the cloth she used to dry herself she wondered when her daughters would return, they must have risen before her and gone out for the morning as she noticed they'd taken bags of food. She pulled on her tunic. From the thick of the trees and deftly hidden, two dark narrow eyes watched....

Night fell quickly in the desert. After jumping the great rift the dawn sun had quietly sent its first rays over the Mountains of Falling Stones. Trotting down into the valley the procession was met with much joy and celebration by the rest of the herd. After each unicorn had retold its story they went to graze. The elders gathered and the King bowed to Dark Fire.

"Sire, I am in your debt, without your help we would never have rescued the unicorns. I am forever grateful."

Dark Fire nickered his reply, "My King, it is the two man-'girls' that found them. Without their help I would not have known where to look." He looked over to where Heather and Olga were standing. They smiled and giggled self consciously. He bowed to them, and the King and all the elders bowed too.

The King continued, "We thank you Heather and Olga. We now must gather our strength, we stay strong, we wait here. I hope that the Beast of Dekserot will leave us alone now, but there is Thoemanny still...." He looked across to Dark Fire. "And the girls, will need to return home."

It was late morning when Spit Fire and Dark Fire reached the edge of the woods near to the Trosban tribe's village.

"We stop here," neighed Spit Fire.

"We can't risk being seen," whinnied Dark Fire. "We will come again soon. Keep watch for Thoemanny, till next time, goodbye."

"Goodbye," they echoed and Heather and Olga set off back through the woods towards their home.

Several weeks passed.

Tonight was the eve of Solas-Taiu. The small shoots of barley, oats and flax the villagers had sown at the spring equinox were now reaching for the sun. On this night, they celebrated the coming of summer; local neighbouring tribes gathered together at Solas Aor, the standing stones of the sun temple, playing music, jumping over fires, challenging each other to acts of bravery. As the night went on, the acts and challenges got wilder and wilder.

The Trosban Chief stood, proudly wearing his tribal headdress, the skull and antlers of a white stag. He held up his staff, "I challenge anyone to pull out a burning log from the fire with their teeth and let the flames burn no mouth nor singe no whisker!"

Tam, a large hairy man, stood up. He stretched his thick arms above his head, extending his huge bulky frame, and let out a loud primal cry. He was bare chested, and covered in a thick mat of hair, so much so that he didn't need skins or cloth to keep warm. A large head of an aurochs tattooed on his shoulders, he was a Tarbrae. He passed the bowl of ceremonial beer to the next man along, Odhar, Heather and Olga's father took it. Sketching a smooth place in the earth beside the fire with his bare feet Tam slowly got down on his knees, lowering his whole body level with the fire and braced himself with his arms bent, crouching on all fours. Staring into the fire for the right moment, he stuck out his head and closed his teeth around a log, easing it out, but the flames danced back towards his face and his beard caught alight. He stood up, dropping the log and covered his face with a hide he'd been sitting on, groaning, more from the shame of failing at the challenge than of the stinging pain at his chin.

Odhar got up, he placed the carved bone bowl down, spilling a little beer, and squatted beside the fire. Chanting and muttering he spat then bent down onto all fours, he stuck out his neck and placed his teeth around the end of a glowing log, dragging it out of the fire. Flames flying from the end of the log clenched in his teeth, he stood up, with outstretched arms and bellowed through his teeth his success. The flames burnt fiercer fanned by the air from his mouth. He dropped the still burning log, coughing and reaching for his beer as he laughed, lapping up his applause. He was then the next to make a challenge.

Odhar stopped laughing and cleared his throat. "I challenge all of you sat here to find a *unicorn*! And cut out its horn while its still alive and bring it here tonight!" The circle of mostly men around the fire went quiet, now the topic had turned serious. Some got up and left for their huts and camps taking this moment for a break. Odhar continued, "I will go! Who's with me?" Ten men got up, swaying, chanting their allegiance. Another two stood. Reaching down for their spears, the party drummed them into the earth, beating a rhythm on the ground. Chanting songs of bravery and skill, they prepared to leave the fireside, energised and intoxicated.

Meanwhile, the younger ones of the tribes were holding their own fireside challenges.

Marl, a boy not much older than Heather, shouted out, "I set a challenge to go swimming in the pools!" The children giggled and mumbled around the circle, both laughing and fierce in their youth. It was a bright, moonlit night but in early summer the pools would be stone cold and nighttime was not a time to be going outside the village alone and unarmed.

Brae stood up, "I'll go! who's with me?"

Fuelled by a serving of beer they all got up and ran off down the hill and through the woods, taking nothing but themselves. Heather and Olga ran with them.

There is only one messenger unicorn born every so many years and only the females are ever messengers. They are blessed with an exceptional quality, a kind of sixth sense, an insight for the herd. Their horns, being highly sensitive, have the power to sense danger and need, good or bad, from far away.

The Messenger Unicorn had lived a great many years. She was honoured and respected in the herd, she had given birth to many foals in her time, though not yet another messenger. She raised her head towards the ridgeway that ran the length of their valley. Her horn ached with a kind of heaviness. A tingling went right from the tip back to her forehead and dwelled there like the weight of a thunderstorm. Without a word she trotted off at speed heading for Heather and Olga's village. She knew this feeling and she knew that her young man-thing friends were in some kind of danger.

Jumping into the tranquil pools, still in their tunics, the children splashed and played in the water though it was very cold. Most quickly got out shivering and dripping wet, and ran raucously back up the hill. Heather and Olga swam a little longer, they waited for each other and were the last to get out. They climbed out of the pool and were scrambling up the bank when they heard a rustle in the undergrowth. Standing still and holding their breath they waited, listening.

Something was watching them. A stir of a leaf, a soft step, the overhanging foliage moved. Suddenly a cave lion jumped out in front of them, snarling.

Heather and Olga screamed out, but their cries were lost to the night, smothered by the shouting from the other children running back up the hillside. Cave lions were savage killers, they had once roamed these hills, but these lions hadn't been seen since before the ice.

A rock came flying over their heads and the lion curled its mouth back, hesitating for a moment.

Then the Messenger crashed through the vegetation and reared up behind the girls.

Heather and Olga ran to the cover of the trees and watched

on, terrified if anything should happen to her.

The lion snarled again. Now at close range he took a swipe at the Messenger, who, veering to the side, missed his blow. He wasn't giving up, he was under some sort of trance, all animals of the sky and forests respected unicorns. This lion did not.

The Messenger reared up again, thrashing her hooves, kicking and plunging down, then rearing again. The lion lashed out with his pad of claws. She shook her mighty head, neighed, and arched her neck. This lion wasn't afraid of her flaying hooves. With one final movement she bent her head down, horn directed at the lion, charged forward and plunged it into his heart. He roared as the horn went in and a strange light lingered in his eyes for a moment then left. He blinked, falling down to the earth. Twitching, his paws dragged at the soil, his sides heaved and were still.

The two sisters looked on, shaking. The Messenger neighed and shook her mane and head, her horn tinged slightly wet and bloody. She pawed the ground, and stood still not once taking her gaze off the lion. Then the lion, though the girls thought him dead, took a long breath in. They saw his chest rise and heard the intake of air and he slowly lifted his head. Steadily but nonchalantly he rose up, he shook his mane, looked up at the Messenger, gave what looked like a smile, and bounded off into the woods. He was cured.

The drunken party of men were moving down the hillside; they ran into the children coming up the path. Angry at them being out in the woods at night, they made hollow threats of chastisement sending them home, then carried on. Nearing the pools they saw the Messenger standing there in a clearing. The lion had gone. On seeing their quarry, they suddenly sobered up and ran silently stealthily through the trees, spears poised.

Several of the older boys that had been swimming ignored their fathers' words and tagged along at a distance, eager for adventure, eager to see what the men were after.

The Messenger, alert to every noise, heard the men approaching, and turned and fled with no time for goodbye. Heather and Olga, hidden by the trees, got up turning around to see their father and the other men running down the hill towards them. Their father, stopping for a breath on seeing them, cursed angrily, but noting they were unharmed ran on after the unicorn with a blood thirsty cry.

They were not alone. Brae stood up from where he'd been crouched, awe in his eyes following the flight of the unicorn. He turned to look back at the girls.

"Such power and strength! I saw it all from when the lion first pounced. I threw the rock which stalled it, but I am no match for a cave lion without my spear... we should get back," he spoke without his usual arrogance, quelled by what he'd just seen.

Heather and Olga exchanged glances. Could Brae be trusted? They looked back and gasped in horror as they watched the Messenger, her creamy white tail stretched out behind her like a flag, galloping fast into the distance, and their own father amongst a mob in hot pursuit set to kill.

Tears staining her cheeks, Olga faced Brae, "You mustn't tell *anyone*!"

Further back and completely camouflaged by the undergrowth lay Thoemanny. He lay still observing the whole thing at a distance, bitterness in his eyes. He turned the throbbing, beating living stone over in his hand, it turned translucent, glimmering with a tiny turquoise light, his training on the cave lion wasted. He put it back in his deer-skin pouch slung round his middle. He had kept hidden when he saw the Messenger, remembering well that time she had broken his leg. And now there were many man around with spears. He stayed hidden.

The revelling continued through the night to see the sun rise. Heather and Olga, sat quietly at the back of the group around the fire, anxiously waiting for the return of the drunken hunting party, praying that the Messenger would have got away and be safe. And what of the cave lion? They hadn't seen lions in this part for ages and that he hadn't been scared of the Messenger. And how she'd driven her horn into his chest, they saw it with their own eyes, and he'd got up, transformed, a calm kitten.

They sat there, hugging their knees, the fire glowed, smoke still drifted up into the sky, the rest of the children, from the very young to the half grown adults, lay around the fire, some half asleep, some singing. The sun clipped its first rays over the horizon, heralding the rise of the new summer dawn. Everyone got up, singing stopped and a quiet ambience spread around the group reaching out their arms to touch the sun.

The hunting party made their way back up the hill, making the top just as the whole of the sun blazed above the horizon, passing between the herald stones, Heather and Olga's father amongst them. They were quiet and subdued, no bloody horn had been got, and they quietly joined the rest of their group around the fire, raising their arms to the sun.

Heather and Olga watched them approaching, relieved at their failure.

Brae watched too. Almost fully trained as a watcher, he knew they wouldn't have given up easily, he knew how much a unicorn was wanted dead. He knew the worth of their horn. Yet he said nothing. From what he'd witnessed with the lion, there was something precious here to be respected. A unicorn horn used on its own had no such healing powers. He would honour his promise to the girls and not say anything of what he saw.

A slow drum beat started up, gradually joined by reed pipes and chanting, growing into a crescendo of music, singing and dancing. The Trosban tribe and the tribes of the area, celebrating the coming of summer and the passage of spring after the long dark winter nights.

No one noticed the youth Marl had not returned.

XI

EYOLAS~GRA

The rain fell when the elders gathered to meet again. Odhar strode across the village centre towards the great hall. Stopping to greet an elder outside, they chatted briefly then ducked under the deerskin hanging across the doorway and went inside. A strong fire burned in a shallow pit in the centre of the hall, the tall flames reaching up far, dominating the room. The smoke curling up to escape through the vent in the apex of the conical thatched roof. Elders, watchers and the Chief all sat cross legged around the fire, their faces glowing orange from the flames.

Greyla held up the sacred carved bowl to Odhar. "Drink," she said and rubbed her weary eyes. Taking the bowl off her he sat down and took a deep draft of the strong barley whisky then passed it to the elder at his side.

The Chief carefully lifted off the unicorn horn that hung

around his neck, holding it up with the point in the tip of the flames. "Solas! Solas! Give me sight!" He took a handful of white and pale lilac crystals and placed them into the top of the horn. "The light." Next he took some charcoal ground to a powder and put it inside, then he took a glowing chunk of birch resin and some glowing charcoal from the elder at his right and placed that inside. "Oh god of the light, I implore you, bring me strength and sight!" The crystals ignited and burnt, the end of the horn a bright explosion of intense light that filled the whole room. The chief took the select herbs that his elder offered, he added them to the mix. It smoked profusely and he put the end of the horn to his face and inhaled deeply. One arm outstretched holding his staff, his eyes rolled and he threw his head back. The ceremonial calling had begun.

Heather got up from feeding the wood hens across from the hall, she put down the basket and called over to Olga.

"They're holding council," said Heather, "they'll be talking about the Messenger, and that poor boy, I want to hear what they say, come on." The girls gave knowing looks to each other. It was forbidden for anyone other than the elders, watchers or the Chief to enter the hall during council. They walked across to the great hall.

The Chief was walking inside the circle of elders and watchers. "Marl's death will not be in vain! Stabbed by a unicorn horn and the very unicorn seen! Although it escaped, we know where it went! We will seek out all the unicorns and KILL THEM!" They all stood up, clamouring in agreement and passion. "We gather every man and youth, we gather the tribes together, we take our spears, axes, clubs, we leave tomorrow at first light!"

Heather and Olga had been peering through the deerskin that hung across the doorway. They exchanged darting glances, then quickly ran off across the central space, past the terraces where they paused and caught their breath.

"Killed by a unicorn? By the Messenger? He can't have been?" Olga exclaimed.

"It can't be! Maybe he fell on his spear? He had followed the hunt they'd said." Heather was dismayed. "And what of the unicorns? If the hunt find their valley they'll all be killed, their minds are set."

"We must warn them!" said Olga. "We'll take Uncle Bran's horses."

"We'll have to leave now! They won't go as fast as the unicorns," said Heather urgently.

They ran down to their cave and gathered a few things, their spear, axe and food. Olga picked up a scrap of hide and took a stick of charcoal from the hearth, she wrote; *'It's not the unicorns ~ we will be safe.'* She placed it where their mother would see it, then hurried across to their uncle's paddock where the horses were kept. No one was around, as the council had ended, talk of the plot to attack the unicorns had got out and everyone had crowded round the great hall wanting to know their role.

Heather took a leather thong and looped it round the neck of a sturdy little grey horse with a pretty face. She led the young mare out through the hazel gate and Olga followed with a dun mare in tow. They crossed another terrace then once through the main gateway of their village they mounted their horses and galloped down the wooded hill and across the plains.

Clouds sped across the skies on this late morning in summer, blown into long trails by a strong wind at their side. The horses galloped on. They couldn't go as fast as the unicorns and the wind had grown fierce, forcing them to slow down. Fighting the storm, manes blown sideways, ears back, wild and with fear in their eyes, the two dusky stocky horses carried Heather and Olga on their mission. The two sisters rode low, bent over close to their horses' backs, their wolfskin fur cloaks wrapped tightly round them, the edges of their cloaks flapping madly to break free, their deerskin bags slung across their backs, the spear and axe in their sheaths bound fast to them.

Jumping the streams that crossed their path had been easy on unicorn-back but these horses were much smaller and found it hard. The streams were too wide and they landed in the water, their legs getting drenched. Once the horses refused to jump and instead waded right through.

At the next stream Olga's horse jumped but stumbled on landing and she fell. She fell on her back but her deerskin pack across her back cushioned her fall and she was not hurt. Her horse, scared by the stumble bolted off. She sat up and called after it, but her horse was gone. Standing, she climbed up behind Heather, shaken but still determined to carry on and reach the unicorns before the hunt party did.

They continued battling the wind when they came to the forest. Though the storm had now moved on and lessened, the trees still creaked and groaned, great branches had been torn from their limbs and trees uprooted, all lay smashed and crashed about them. Walking through the devastated forest, creaking branches overhead, they carefully picked their way. Then, through the noise of the wind they heard something moving nearby. They stopped, stricken with fear, and looked, but whatever it was, was hidden by the broken branches. Olga reached for her spear and Heather her axe telling her horse to move on, but her horse stubbornly refused to go ahead. A bow cracked and the creature in the branches moved and they froze, spear raised, axe gripped in defence. Then the creature whinnied, the girls relaxed. It was Olga's horse. The mare stepped out of her cover of fallen trees and both horses walked forward and nuzzled each other. Olga jumped down checking if her horse was hurt, grateful to see her. She looked well, if a little spooked, and Olga climbed back up on her. They carried on through the forest. It was difficult going with all the broken debris strewn across their path and they were very glad when they saw the faint glow in the rocks ahead, the entrance to the Glowing Caves.

They made their way through its tunnels, they crossed the ever changing river and they came out into the unicorns' valley. The wind had died and they had made it.

The valley was filled with sunshine, unicorns grazing peacefully, yet tomorrow this peace would be destroyed. By man. Man-things. Their own tribe.

They somberly, but with a sense of urgency, trotted across the grassy plain, they must find the King, the Messenger, Spit Fire or Dark Fire. It wasn't long before they were spotted and unicorns began to trot towards them, the Messenger cantered up.

"Heather, Olga!" she exclaimed. She read their faces, now broken out in tears. Their horses bowing their heads in greeting.

"You must go," Heather weeped, "the tribes are coming to attack! They know where you ran to, they blame you for the death of a boy." Both girls had tears streaming down their faces.

The King, Spit Fire and Dark Fire came cantering up to the group gathered round the two girls.

The King spoke first, "What is this?"

The girls sobbing, retold what they had overheard from the Trosban elders. The unicorns gathered closer.

It was decided. The unicorns would not leave their valley. They did not want to leave and they had nowhere else to go. They would stand their ground and defend their land. The easiest and most direct way in was through the Glowing Caves, here they would stand guard and watch. The other ways to their valley, across the treacherous Mountains of Falling Stones or scaling the great ridge that ran parallel along the length of their valley, seemed unlikely.

The unicorns wanted to prove their innocence. They needed Heather and Olga to show they wished man-things no harm. And they needed to find the real killers...Thoemanny and Dekserot.

"Trosbans, Tarbraes, Arthruades, Iolaires and Cabhairs," the Trosban Chief shouted, raising his voice to address the crowd above the noise of the wind. "We gather together! We fight together! We will defeat the unicorns! And our tribes can live and prosper without the fear of these creatures!" A mass of men and youths of all the tribes in the area had gathered together inside the Trosban tribe's village, carrying spears, axes, clubs and anything that could be used as a weapon, adding to those that had stayed behind after the Solas-Taiu celebrations. A few elders of the tribes carried the rare and valuable unicorn horns. Some rode horses, some on foot, it was a riot of noise and mud, the ground churned up by the many feet and hooves. The wind raged on.

The Trosban Chief spoke again. "Half will go through the Caves of Light, they lead directly to the unicorns' land. Half will climb the Crumbling Mountains beyond the caves and attack from the other side. We'll surround the unicorns and kill them, we will wipe them out so they can kill us at night no more! And we will cut out their precious valuable horns while they lie dying in the dust! We will have horns to trade with far lands! We will triumph!" There was a loud uprising from the crowd, calling out in agreement, unity and lust for blood. The noise like a great seething mass, an angry mob. Each tribe had lost something or someone to 'the unicorns' or so it was believed. All had died in the same way, a stab from a unicorn horn, be it deer, dog or man. The talks continued late into the evening and all this time Heather and Olga's mother sat reading and rereading the scratched note left on the piece of deerskin.

Dark Fire neighed, taking over from the King, addressing the group. "We have to go back to the sea caves. Dekserot has become Thoemanny's pet, I believe we will find them there. We must bring them here and show them to the man-things. It's our only hope. We talk to them, make an oath with them, bind them captive or kill them if we have to. But we need them." He paced the ground. "Myself and Spit Fire will go, you are all needed here to defend our land. Olga, Heather, you come too. You are invaluable and when we return you show the man-things we will not harm them unless they harm us. Time is short. Get on our backs, we leave now." Heather and Olga obediently climbed upon Spit Fire and Dark Fire's backs. No one wanted bloodshed. They had to face the beasts to bring peace. The unicorns reared, flicked their tails and turned, galloping off like a flash of light.

Dawn had not yet risen and the tribes had packed up their camp. And they left, leaving their fires smoking, the ground churned up, and the women unsettled. Most of the women and children stayed behind to look after the animals and crops, the babies and young children. It was an anxious time. No one knew how many unicorns there were, no one knew how many of the hunt party would return.

They travelled through the night, the girls sleeping across the unicorns' backs, they didn't wake when they jumped the crack, the great rift that crunched time and twisted it to its own desire. They slept on. When Heather opened her eyes the sun beat down on a glistening sea on the horizon. Sea birds were flying inland, circling above their heads, squawking and complaining, complaining that their peaceful cliff top homes had been disturbed by a great clumsy beast...Dekserot. Dark Fire and Spit Fire listened to their cries.

"Where is this?" Dark Fire called out to the birds.

"On the Island, the Island, the cliffs on the Island, the Spirit Island in the sea out there," the birds all cried in repetition.

Dark Fire flew up amongst the birds where he could see further out to sea. Olga clung on, she had definitely now woken up. The clamour of the birds, the bright sun and the fresh air filled her with energy. Flying towards the Island it looked like an ancient causeway joined it to the mainland. The tide was far out and revealed a stoney bed raised up to form a pathway through the saltmarsh.

"The Spirit Island?" echoed Spit Fire, as Dark Fire rejoined them.

"Yes?" nickered Dark Fire.

"As in the Tunnels of Spirits?" replied Spit Fire. "On an island beyond the Mountains of Falling Stones?" Dark Fire looked blank. Spit Fire shook his mane and whinnied, giving a fearful waring look. "We don't want to go there at night."

The sun was high in the sky and shone brilliantly down upon them, night seemed a long way off. They cantered along the cliff tops, passing the old volcano that Dark Fire had disturbed, still quietly smoking, and beyond to the next

111

headland that jutted out to sea. There the cliffs fell away swallowed by sand dunes which turned wet and marshy. A narrow spit of sand wound its way out of the marsh and joined the stoney causeway across to the Island.

The hunt party had been gone half a day. Heather and Olga's mother, Eyolas-Gra, was gathering water mint and wild garlic down by the base of the waterfall near their village. She took handfuls and placed them in her woven reed basket. The water tumbled and rushed into the stream as she moved down the bank.

'...*hmm, mo onam cara, is tu mo gra, ...my soul mate, you are my love ...hmm,*' she hummed and sang a melody to herself, taking her mind off the fact that her daughters hadn't returned.

She focussed on gathering herbs, the woodland calls and the colours around her; brilliant green mosses covered the rocks and little silver fish darted in the stiller waters of the pools near the bank. The noise of the waterfall covered the birdsong and the hum of the insects in the trees. It covered the other noises in the woods nearby. It masked the footsteps of a dark shape that moved in the undergrowth alongside her, monitoring every move she made.

She stopped, hesitating and stood up, a handful of herbs in her hand, she thought she had heard something. The sun shone brightly through the overhanging branches, a bird flew high overhead, the stream rushed on, the waterfall crashed and cascaded into the pool. Everything was normal but she felt a cold unease, something was watching her....

In two steps, steps that she unmistakably heard, it was behind her, clawed hand on her shoulder, clawed hand on her arm. A guttural sound, a cough, a wheeze, ...dragging her back!

With a sudden twist and a knee in his groin, she was free!

112

Running, running for her life. Thoemanny hard on her tail. Behind her like a shadow, he chased. She ran and ran, following the banks of the stream, and on into the woods. She ran, stumbled, ran, tree roots, rocks, branches caught her hair, she ran on. Claws grazed her arm, he was so close, he wheezed, she gained a pace, she stumbled, he caught up, a large root came up, she stumbled again, falling full on the earth.

He fell on her with his whole bulk and weight, his sweat running down her neck. He seized her arm and turned her over, stopping her escape with his force. His face, close to hers, breathing laboured. In those dark eyes she saw a savage desperation, a hurting, of age and loss and broken dreams.

In her eyes he saw a memory, of his mate he lost many years ago. He lifted her hair that clung to her cheek from her tears and flight. Red and rust coloured, the same as his mates, and his pups, long gone now, starved in the ice. A tear rolled down his face. With a single claw he delicately followed the outline of her face from her temple down to her neck, it was not his mate, he must let her go, he had no wish to harm her. He felt compassion for her and the two girls that had led him to her, and he released his grip. Torn between the overwhelming instinct to survive and haunted by the memory of his past. He stood up, over her, threw his great head back and screamed at the sky, a dark and rasping scream, he turned and strode off smashing his way through the trees not caring if he was heard.

XII

THE TUNNELS OF
SPIRITS

The tide was still a long way out as Heather and Olga and the unicorns cantered across the hard stone causeway. Its surface aged, old and worn, angular stones with deep cracks weathered by the tide, an ancient way, built up from ages past. Its stony embankments reached out and joined the tall sculpted cliffs of the Island. Sea birds circled, flying to their cliffside nests and back out to sea, diving into the deep waters for fish to bring back to their hungry chicks.

The two girls and the unicorns walked along the cliffs on the Island, to one side the rock dropped away dramatically into the sea and to the other lay the heart of the island, lush and green, with undulating hills and tall majestic trees. It felt alive and exciting, not at all threatening or foreboding as Spit Fire implied. They looked for evidence of the Beast of Dekserot, but found none.

After a while they came to a large opening, a gash, in the hillside away from the cliffs, cautiously they approached it.

"It is said the mouth of the Tunnels of Spirits is like a gaping wound in the hillside," neighed Spit Fire. "There is a legend that tells of a huge chamber within the tunnels where the spirits go at night, and after dark, no adventurer or traveller has ever returned." He looked back up at the sun in the sky assuring himself that it wasn't setting anytime soon.

"Come on then, a likely hide out for the last of the dragoss," Dark Fire whinnied fearlessly trotting forward.

Entering the mouth was like stepping into another world. Huge limestone stalagmites and stalactites had joined together to form thick pillars of white, like the teeth in the jaws of some creature of the hillside.

Inside it was cool and echoey and chilling. They stood, their eyes adjusting to the dark, the cave became long and narrow at one end, and disappeared into black. Suddenly there came a high pitched screeching noise, sharp and unbearable. They covered their ears. Whatever it was it sounded in distress. They rushed outside.

A great grey bird was hovering low in the sky at the mouth of the cave. Its huge wings outstretched wide, each wing twice the length of Heather and Olga. It swooped down suddenly, letting out another piercing cry then flew back up. And then dived down again, just missing their heads.

"I remember," whinnied Dark Fire, "it is the fire bird that took me as a colt and dropped me in the crack in the desert. Where its talons gripped my body I grew wings...." he gazed up at the bird, transfixed as the memory flashed back.

The bird came swooping down again, crying out to Dark

115

Fire. He shook his mane. "It, it's in distress. I think it wants us to follow it." And he started to canter off after it as it soared away. Spit Fire and Heather followed, a little unsure.

The bird flew across the Island, over the rocks and hills, they followed. It stopped then began to circle a large tree. Dark Fire flew up to see why the bird had stopped. The tree was wide and old, its great trunk all hollowed out in the centre, and there in the centre of the tree was a kind of nest and in that nest lay a gigantic egg. Dark Fire flew back down, the bird swooped and landed beside him, giving that same piercing shrill call, Dark Fire neighed in reply.

"There is a gigantic egg inside the tree! This bird wants us to help crack it open," he explained to the others, who couldn't understand what was said. Stepping around the tree and due to it being hollow, they could all see the egg snuggly resting on a bed of small branches and twigs and soft down. The girls got off the unicorns' backs to climb up to it and marvelled at the egg's size. It suddenly shook and they jumped back a step.

"Yes, it needs to hatch. It can't do it on its own. The shell has grown too tough," Dark fire whinnied. Heather and Olga tapped it with their knuckles, it was solid, so they looked nearby for a sharp rock, and Heather took out her axe. Gently at first they tapped it, then as these attempts were futile they steadily used more force. The egg was tightly tucked away inside the bowels of the tree and Spit Fire and Dark Fire could not reach it to help crack the shell. They left it to the girls.

Heather cracked one more blow with her axe, cracking the shell and breaking through so that a small hole appeared. They tapped away and the hole grew bigger until the shell lay completely smashed and open to the world. And inside the egg lay not a bird as they expected to see, but a small horse. Perfectly formed, the small horse opened its eyes and gazed at the bewildered figures looking over it. Two small wings lay folded back against its sides. A shiver ran down its slate blue-grey coat and it shook its fine fluffy mane, singed with a cobalt hue, that stuck up along its neck. Heather and Olga stared in amazement. The horse was beautiful and exquisite, yet unnatural and haunting. Olga noticed a blue-grey feather bud growing just behind its ears, and pointed it out to Dark Fire. Dark Fire stretched out his muzzle and sniffed the little horse, who reached up its nose to touch Dark Fire.

Dark Fire snorted, "I think this is a feather horse. Very rare, unheard of, only in legends. From a time of the old knowledge...." his thoughts trailed off. The large fire bird came down and thrust its beak at the horse which instinctively opened its mouth and the bird proceeded to regurgitate some green delight. It squawked again, speaking to Dark Fire, then flew off. Dark Fire blew gently down his nostrils nickering to the horse and she whinnied back.

"Her name is Penna," nickered Dark Fire, "she does not understand the language of man-things as we do." And the little foal tentatively tried to stand.

The sun drew in its shadows, slipping into the horizon, disappearing through the trees. Eyolas stumbled back to the village badly shaken. She sought out some of the other women and told of her attack. They gathered round her listening intently, Greyla the elder, was amongst them, she rubbed the top of her staff with her thumb, a look of contempt crossed her face.

"And your children gone? Tooken off with our Bran's horses? At a time like this when *every* horse is needed!" her old frame shook as she leant on her staff, accusingly.

Shocked at Greyla's heartless response, Eyolas retorted,

"They are good girls. They will bring the horses back."

Greyla grumbled raising her voice, "But they took without asking! Eyyyr, They cause trouble!"

Exasperated and tearful, Eyolas continued, "They must have good reason! And they could be lost or hurt!"

"Serve them right," Greyla stared coldly at Eyolas and rubbed her eye with her free hand.

Eyolas fumbled in her pouch and took out Olga's message on the scrap of hide. She unfolded it and thrust it at the old woman.

"And there's this!" she challenged. The other women moved closer. Greyla was a much respected elder. She'd led hunts in her day when there were still many bears in the land. Now she spoke with the gods and interpreted their signs, and she harboured her suspicions of Heather and Olga and their association with unicorns.

Greyla read out the marks of Olga's message to the group of gathered women, threw the scrap of hide on the ground and spat. "Unicorns!" The other women stared, they were not sure whether Eyolas was raving or telling the truth. And they started to move away, calling to their children, to keep them close, safe behind the gates and ditches of the village.

Eyolas felt drained and cut off. Her respected place as a watcher's woman knocked down by Greyla's words, and she worried about her daughters. She picked up Olga's message and left, tears streaming down her face, determined to look for them at first light.

Thoemanny, after his initial anger had subsided, had stopped in his reckless rampage and turned. He had followed the mother's tracks back up to the watchers' caves and there he lay in the shadows waiting and watching. The slim figure of the mother returned, walking slowly, the last rays of light glowing orange on her wet face. He reached into his pouch and closed his clawed fist around the living stone nestled there. Bringing it up to his face he closed his lips onto it whispering low, muttering deep tones, never once taking his eyes off the figure at the cave door.

Standing before her doorway Eyolas paused, that same prickly feeling crawling up the back of her neck. The undergrowth rustled, she turned round abruptly, she was sure she had closed the gates behind her? She heard a faint tink, and then a small round stone rolled against her foot. She bent down and picked it up, once in her hands, it came alive, shining bright, a crystal, a deep blue and violet in its heart, it was mystifying and hypnotising. It felt strangely warm in her grasp and she felt she could not put it down. She turned it slowly round in her hands, and instinctively put it up to her face, pressed it against her lips and stared into its depths. She looked closer. She thought she saw an eye, just one eye, a closed eye, with long black lashes and a shadow underneath, lying deep within the crystal's core. It opened, a dark eye that looked into her soul, she knew that eye, it was the eye of her attacker, the monster, the beast. She stared, and blinked, it couldn't be, it must be a trick of the light. Then it came back to her. The beast, standing over her, horns clinking, swinging from a band around his middle, as he threw back his head and roared. ...Swinging horns.... Unicorn horns? She dropped the stone and stood there shaking, peering into the ever increasing dusk. It must have been a flash back. Assuring herself there was nothing there, she glanced across at where the stone had rolled to, it could be valuable, she could trade it, it was beautiful and alluring, finding it had made her feel special. She walked over to the stone, it lay on the earth its sparkling light now dulled, she picked it up. Now strangely cold in her palm, she turned it round, a tiny red glow, deep at its core, seemed to beat, once more she felt its strange magnetic energy and she couldn't stop looking at it. She held it close to her chest, she would keep it and she would keep it hidden. This would be her secret. A sign from the gods. She entered the cave. Unknowingly to her the living stone had begun its possession.

Thoemanny left the watchers' caves. He crept through the undergrowth silently, he had to return to the unicorns that he'd left guarded by the Beast of Dekserot. He had watched the many man arrive and avoided the way they'd travelled, instead moving up through the Forest of Eagla on the flanks of the Mountains of Falling Stones, a more difficult route, but then making his way through the desert and on to the sea.

The sun had fallen low in the sky over the Island so the four travellers took shelter near the hollow tree. Heather and Olga made a fire and sat round it sharing a meal of dried fish, nut bread, and fruit, with water they'd brought carried in a skin. The unicorns grazed on the lush grass nearby and Penna slept in her nest. When dusk fell the bird flew off and did not return.

Morning came, they gathered their things ready to set off to find the two beasts, Penna whinnied, stumbling and trotting after them. With the great fire bird not seen since the evening, Dark Fire flew up and searched from the skies but he could see no sign of it. He flew down and spoke with Penna, although she could now stand on her legs, she was still just a day old, and Dark Fire feeling a responsibility to keep her safe, reluctantly let her follow.

They entered the mouth. Dark Fire led, Spit Fire behind,

Heather and Olga walked beside them, carrying torches fashioned from split branches, and Penna followed.

They entered the blackness. A long winding tunnel took them into the earth, strange noises echoed around them, Heather and Olga looked at each other, spear and axe held firmly, holding their torches up at the smooth rock walls.

Thoemanny let out a roar and sank to his knees. He had reached the dormant crater where he'd left Dekserot and his captive unicorns and he threw his fists on the floor and howled in anguish at his loss. He swayed his great heavy head and grabbed his horns as if to tear them out. All his life he had hunted unicorns, like his fathers before him, and now, with his family dead and faced with being the last of his kind, he had wanted to prove to himself that he was still great. He could tame the dragoss, the Beast of Dekserot, he knew how to work with living stones, he loved to challenge power, like the Beast of Bas-Taibhse, that would have been his but that it died a terrible death. He rose up from his knees. Anger rising up inside him. He must find Dekserot and the unicorns.

Coming round a bend in the tunnel the girls, unicorns and Penna found themselves in a large chamber. Off it lay several other tunnels, enshrouded with blackness.

"This must be the Chamber of Spirits," said Spit Fire, "we must keep the torches alight."

"I thought you said it was just at night the spirits come out?" queried Heather anxiously.

"Yes, but I can't be sure," whinnied Spit Fire nervously. Their torch light dancing up the high rock walls. The earth on the floor of the chamber had been churned up, Dark Fire lowered his head and sniffed.

121

"Dekserot has been here recently," he quietly nickered. Just then they heard something running. Heavy steps, quick and running towards them, running from where they'd come. Then they could hear thick breathing, heavy and laboured, and muttering to itself, a deep guttural tone they all recognised too well. They pressed their backs against the wall and gripped their weapons. The unicorns standing, heads lowered to meet their foe.

Thoemanny roared. Long and low and twisted. This was his time now. His roar echoed down the tunnels and came back sounding like a different roar. He stepped out into the chamber, his broad bulk outlined by the torchlight, he let out a tremendous growl and spoke in Heather and Olga's language....

"Are you ready for a challenge? Unicorn of Fire and Dark? Unicorn of Spitting Fire? I will rip out your horns and eat your flesh and take your *pets,*" looking at the two sisters, "I already have their mother at my will...." Thoemanny's gravelly voice trailed off.

Shocked to hear Thoemanny use their language and frightened by what he said about their mother, not their mother! The girls confronted the beast.

"No!" shouted Heather.

"What have you done with our mother? She is at your *will*? What do you mean?" spoke out Olga, terrified.

Thoemanny smiled and growled, "I am possessing her. And she does not even know it! ...at my will and at my command."

Olga shrieked and charged with her spear, and Heather screaming, jumped forward wielding her axe. Thoemanny laughed and grabbed their weapons, spinning them round to use himself. Dark Fire jumped forward to protect the girls, brandishing his horn and arching his wings, just as another deeper roar boomed through the tunnels... and the shadow of the Beast of Dekserot crossed the floor.

Dark Fire stepped out to confront the beasts. "Yes, so be it this way!" He knew he had power, he knew he had five lives, but he knew this was his last. He shut his eyes for a moment, concentrating his horn, fire sparking from the end of it. Thoemanny laughed again. Dark Fire charged, reared up and smashed his hooves down, Thoemanny twisting out of the way.

The Beast of Dekserot roared again, breathed a blast of fire and came running into the chamber, writhing as he ran from side to side like a great lizard. He lurched forward with open jaws, a mass of teeth, wet and jagged, he swung at Dark Fire who swiftly jumped to the side, taking a bite of only air. Spit Fire reared up and struck out at Thoemanny, this time landing a glancing blow on his shoulder. Thoemanny recoiled, and threw himself back at the fight fuelled with more aggression from the pain. The noise of growls, neighs and roars, of clashing hooves on rock and flesh, of claws on hides and beating wings filled the tunnels, and the shadows and shapes of the seething mass continued.

Penna could not watch, and Heather and Olga held their breath.

Dekserot screamed, and reaching out with his neck and teeth tore at Dark Fire's coat and, as Dark Fire twisted in mid flight, Dark Fire struck down hard with his hoof on Dekserot's eye. The dragoss ran off whimpering, back down one of the tunnels. Dark Fire paused to pursue him then turned to face Thoemanny with Spit Fire.

Spit Fire was tiring, Dark Fire charged at Thoemanny who threw himself onto Dark Fire, sinking his teeth into his throat. He ripped his mouth away.

The sisters cried out, "No!"

Dark Fire, a great tear at his throat, collapsed to the floor.

123

Thoemanny stood over him and roared long and loud, deep from his belly.

The torches went out.

Spit Fire and the girls gasped, too stunned to move. It was total blackness.

Then the spirits came.

Distant eyes glowing and growing bigger, of many colours, coming from all the tunnels into the chamber, a thin trail of light dust following them. A sad wailing echoing round the rock walls. They surrounded Dark Fire.

The figures in the chamber were illuminated by the faint light they emitted, and there he lay, not breathing, his last life spent. Spit Fire, the girls, Thoemanny, all froze and held their breath. These were the spirits, dark spirits, bad spirits... Spit Fire knew what legends told. No one moved. The spirits settled above Dark Fire, their wailing becoming a throbbing crescendo and they began to circle above him. Then they were suddenly silent and dropped and fell upon him like dust, a light-glowing dust.

Moments passed that seemed like hours.

Stillness.

Then, a slight movement.

And Dark Fire raised his head and snorted the dust out of his nostrils.

Thoemanny, seeing the work of the spirits shrank back in awe of his foe.

Dark Fire lived again. The dark spirits sending him back. Yet with no more lives left.

There was an unnatural lull.

"Think I'm scared of a few dark spirits!" Thoemanny rushed forward again, thrusting Olga's spear ahead of him, but Spit Fire reared and knocked it away with his hooves, only for

Thoemanny to throw the axe at him which he narrowly missed, sliding away across the floor.

Dark Fire stood up, regaining his strength. The tear at his neck now just a scratch.

"I am Dark Fire!" he neighed. "Power over darkness and power over fire." And he reared up screaming at Thoemanny.

The unicorn and the beast tore at each others coats, Dark Fire shrieking and Thoemanny yelling hoarsely. They both tired. With one last effort, Thoemanny grabbed Dark Fire around his head, pulling him down. Dark Fire shook himself and broke free of Thoemanny's grip and lowered his head to charge, summoning fire from his horn. But just at that moment the Beast of Dekserot came thundering back into the fray, blasting out a carpet of fire and jumped at Dark Fire tearing a gash in his side and knocking him down to the ground.

Spit Fire reared up in his defence. Thoemanny turned to run, but Dark Fire stuck out his leg and tripped him up sending him crashing to the ground. Then with enormous effort Dark Fire raised his mighty head and got up. Standing over Thoemanny he lowered his head and stuck his horn deep into Thoemanny's heart.

Thoemanny writhed and let out a bloody roar, all the breath seeping out of him. He gripped Dark Fire's horn as it penetrated his chest pulling it in deeper, his eyes so suddenly old, he knew he had lost and he welcomed death like an old friend, sad and defeated, the last of his line.

Seeing Thoemanny dead, Dekserot fled.

Heather and Olga rushed to Dark Fire's side alarmed at the deep gashes in his thigh, blood running down his leg.

Olga was distraught with anger at the beasts, at how they had hurt Dark Fire. She reached down to the Beast of Thoemanny's head, tears streaming down her cheeks, and grabbed one of his great horns and wrenched at it to tear it off. There was a ripping sound, a cord broke and both horns came away in her hand attached to a headdress, joining the spikes along his back sewn to his hide.

Underneath revealed his head covered in matted hair, and small ears like a mans. He was a man. A man-thing. A giant man. A giant man of an old race. The last.

XIII

DEKSEROT

The morning was bright on the next day and Eyolas awoke to birdsong. She had slept long and deeply, she got up and re-lit the fire throwing some extra wood and charcoal on it. She placed a pottery bowl in the fire, filled with deer milk and ground roasted dandelion root. She glanced at the stone that she'd come to possess last night and picked it up turning it over in her hand. Holding it in front of the fire it shone a brilliant turquoise, the flames of the fire danced through it, refracted into many shapes by its crystal shakes. She looked closer, the crystal shakes began to move and drifted together becoming an eye, there it was again, faint, but it was no trick of her imagination. The dark eye opened and looked back at her, distantly, sad, its depths like a dark pool, the corners welled up with wet and a tear trickled down and dripped from the stone and onto the floor....

Without his master the Beast of Dekserot was lost. Running from the tunnels of spirits he had not stopped, he'd reached the Mountains of Falling Stones and collapsed, hungry, exhausted and injured. His old haunt, his home. He found a rocky shelter and rested, waiting for nightfall when he would go searching for food and water.

The hunt party had split. It had taken them till nightfall to reach the entrance to the Glowing Caves, there they'd made camp and in the first light of morning it was decided who would go into the mountains and who would go through the cave system. Thirty men, four women and five horses were chosen to climb the Mountains of Falling Stones. Most were from the Trosbans and Iolaires who had the best climbers, and some from the Cabhairs. They'd taken ropes made from honeysuckle and nettle and their most sure footed horses to carry their water, food and weapons. It was a long day, an arduous climb. The sun beat down on them as they made their ascent, reflecting harshly off the pale crumbling rocks, rocks would come away in their hands as they inched along narrow ledges and pulled themselves over rocky promontories. Odhar was amongst the group of climbers, with Brae close behind him. By late afternoon they reached a small plateau and rested. From here the going got easier and after resting and eating they continued on up.

Through the tunnels of the Glowing Caves the rest of the hunt party made their way, led by the Trosban Chief. They crossed the ever changing river one at a time with ropes, as it was flowing fast and high, and they soon came to the opening into the unicorns' valley. The long beautiful valley lay still and empty. It looked deserted. Cautiously the warriors moved outside. They didn't feel the eyes watching them as they left the shelter of the caves and began to make their way across the valley plain.

Over half way up the Mountains of Falling Stones, the climbers, tired and hot, continued on at a slower pace.

On the mountain the beast awakened.... Dekserot lifted his large scaly head and flared his nostrils, he'd slept for a while and something had woken him. He smelt man-thing. Strong and sweaty, a steady breeze bringing their smell directly to him. His stomach ached, his mouth salivated.

Dinner.

Death of his master.

Man-things had brought the unicorns, and death.

He saw red. An uncontrollable rage. Silently and breathing fast he stealthily writhed out of his rocky shelter.

They heard it coming, but too late to run, the great dragon-like beast sprung upon them, breathing fire. The tall man from the Iolaires leading the party of climbers, spread his legs wide for stability and poised his spear. But the beast reached down its neck and grabbed him in its jaws, crunching his body like an apple and throwing his broken mess down like a rotten core. A piercing growl, a roar, and it had taken another, tossing the ripped body across the rocks. Screaming and shouting, the hunt party had flung themselves apart, grabbing what weapons they could, though they had not been prepared, believing the dragons of old had long died. From pinions of safety behind rocks they fired arrows and threw spears, none could penetrate its skin, all fell flat on the rocks, bouncing off the beast's thick scales that covered its body like an armour of stone. It roared at them and went in to attack, taking one more, a youth, from his perch.

Odhar was trapped on a ledge in reach of the swaying jaws of the beast. Brae, seeing this from the rock below, aimed his spear and threw it hard, catching the beast's soft palette at the side of its jaw. It shrieked, stopping at the annoying prick in its gum. In that moment Odhar jumped from the ledge and grabbed Brae's arm. What was left of the hunt fled.

In a blind rage Dekserot came after them, the hunter becoming the hunted. They ran and fell, falling back down the steep slopes of the mountain. Dekserot close behind them, picking them off like flies and tossing them aside, he stopped suddenly, seeing the way down too steep for him. Scrabbling to get a grip, tearing at the rocks, he regained his balance and lifted his head, roaring in defiance, blood dripping from his jaws, and went back to feed....

Back in the valley the hunters stopped, hearing a distant roar, like thunder, in the mountains. The unicorns heard. They knew that terrible sound. They remained hidden in the tall grasses.

Less than half the climbers made it back down the mountain. And those that did were injured. They ran on, stumbling, exhausted, not sure if the beast was still behind them, not daring to pause long enough to look back, making their way through the caves to warn the others of this dragon-like beast in the mountains that was on a killing rampage. Odhar had fractured his wrist on falling, but he was alive, he staggered on through the tunnels in desperation.

In the valley the hunters crept low. Finally, the Messenger could wait no longer, her horn was aching, all the unicorns had seen and smelt the man-things from a long way off, yet she sensed more danger rising from far beyond the valley. She raised her head, nickering to the others standing with her, the elders, Solas, Saor and Samant.

The hunters saw and all fifty or more stood up tall, aiming their fine sharp arrows and flint tipped spears at the unicorns they faced. They drew back their long yew bows.

The King, the Messenger, the elders, and the herd standing behind them, all rose up tall on their hind legs and screamed at the man-things to put down their spears and bows. But the man-things did not hear, to them it sounded like a frightening scream.

They released their arrows.

The unicorns charged.

The hunters ran with their spears and charged on horseback and screamed an attack as the arrows fell.

Many hit and many fell.

Yet the unicorns carried on, arrows stuck in them, charging fast till they hit the hunters like a wall of bludgeoning hooves. Men fell. Their horses reared and threw them.

The Trosban Chief, leading the charge took his spear and charged at the Messenger. The King, seeing this, swooped down, wings open, fanned out, threatening, reared up screaming at the man. His hooves came down on top of the Chief. The Chief swerved, missing the Messenger, her hoof glancing a blow to his head, falling backwards, spear raised, he gripped it hard and thrust it out, into the belly of the King....

Odhar shouted hoarsely from across the valley, "Stop! Stop! Retreat! There's a dragon-beast attacking! He has killed many of us! He will come here! We can not win. Save our souls and

131

retreat! Retreat!"

The other men and Brae joined in, running towards the battle, shouting, "Retreat!"

The men in the valley stopped, and looked back.

As if to confirm their claims the mountains roared again, this time louder and nearer, from the forest edges at the foothills of the mountains, at the end of the valley. They saw the horror and blood stains on the faces of the returning men. They turned. And they retreated back, towards them.

And the screeching roar got louder. The Beast of Dekserot, driven by madness, loss and an unbridled desire for blood, entered the valley, writhing skittish as he zigzagged his way across the plain.

The Messenger cried out. The King lay bleeding with a spear in his underside. She stood by his side. Slowly, she moved her head and neck in the direction of the beast. She felt unbelievably sad, numb to the wounded men at her feet, crawling their way back across the valley towards the caves. The other unicorns gathered around her. She lifted her hoof, hesitating, poised, all her energy focussed on the beast fast approaching her. The early evening sun highlighted her flowing mane brilliantly, iridescently, lifting in the breeze. Yet underneath she was a tight thunderbolt, every muscle tensed, waiting for the right moment.

Slowly she lowered her head, horn pointed, eyes on the beast. And she charged. A sleek flash, a streak of golden light, like a shining arrow she charged.

Dekserot running onwards, breathing his fiery breath, tried to lean away and avoid her horn, while rearing up on his hind legs and reaching round to grab her neck in his jaws. He howled as her horn went in under his foreleg. His teeth grazed her neck, sinking into her flesh but then loosening, not gripping, as he recoiled in pain. The other unicorns caught up and reared, their hooves crashing down on him. Dekserot growled, gruelling and roaring. He backed away. Injured badly and the unicorns too much for him. Turning he ran, bleeding, back to the mountains.

The hunters had watched, terrified, in awe, unable to run, transfixed by what they saw. The dragon-beast, the vision the Trosban Chief had seen in the fire, come to life. But the unicorns attacked it? Watching the beast flee the men then fled, back through the tunnels of the Glowing Caves, not stopping to rest, they carried who they could, the fastest and ablest went on ahead.

Brae looked back for a moment, he felt a pang of deep shame at the fallen unicorn.

Dark Fire had rested a day on the Island. Olga and Heather had collected yarrow, elfwort and oak leaves, herbs they could find easily around them, herbs to bind and heal his wounds. Crushing the leaves in their hands Olga carefully applied them, mixing the herbs with clays from the cliffs to help them stick. When Dark Fire felt well enough to eat and drink, they left for home. Penna left with them, she was grazing on grass the same as the unicorns and the bird had not returned. They collected their packs, their axe and spear, filled their skin with fresh water, and tied on the Beast of Thoemanny's headdress and his band of unicorn horns.

Darkness was drawing in and there was no moon, but they could wait no longer, Dekserot was raging and unpredictable, they imagined he would travel back to his old haunts close to the herd and there was the threat from the man-tribe. They cantered in silence and solemnity, fearful for the time they'd spent away.

By the time they reached the Mountains of Falling Stones, the night had swept its cloak across the land and it was pitch black. Dark Fire's wound was weeping and bleeding again, they stopped high up on a plateau sheltered on one side by a tall rock face where they rested a short while and Olga redressed his wound. They had brought the torches they made before along with them, ready stuffed with kindling and a swab of resin, they lit them now with Dark Fire's help, it was not safe carrying on without them on the treacherous mountain terrain.

The hunters ran through the night, their horses exhausted, a third of their men, youths and women had been lost. The Trosban Chief had sustained a bad blow to his head from the Messenger's hoof, and was carried back lain across his horse. They reached their homelands in darkness, holding few flaring torches through the welcome woodlands of hazel and oak, they staggered up and to their gates, heralding their arrival by blowing on a long horn, made from an aurochs.

Once inside they fell down and collapsed, their women risen from their beds, rushed to their sides. All the tribes took refuge for the rest of the night.

Their story unfolded. A garbled mix of events in no order. Eyolas-Gra stroked her man's hair, she wanted to tell him her anguish of their daughters disappearance and of her attack, but he had gone straight out from the meeting to the hunt before she could tell him the night they'd gone. Yet now she hesitated, afraid that he would blame her.

After eating and drinking, the ones that were well held an emergency council in the great hall. The women of the village attended too, and the elders, watchers and chiefs of each tribe, and the rest of the hunt party.

Odhar stood up and began. The Trosban Chief was slouched on some furs, propped up to listen.

"Our party split, one half went through the caves and the other up the mountains. It was in the mountains where we met with a terrible dragon-beast. Like the dragons of old. It tore our party apart, massacred us, thrown about like rotten fruit. I was there. We got away but not without our losses. We returned to the others, to warn them. They had been badly attacked by the unicorns, but no fatalities. Our Chief killed a large grey winged unicorn, a stallion. He received his blow to his head at that time. We could not take any horns, we had to return as the dragon came down after us. The dragon could come here and attack our home! And the unicorns too!"

Brae interrupted, "You saw them attack the dragon-beast! You all saw them...?"

Odhar cut him short and carried on, "Our defences would not last. This beast has to be destroyed. We build a pit and drive it into it, like our ancestors did. We need the unicorns! We need their horns, we need to take their horns! The *only* weapon that can penetrate the thick scales of the beast! We gather our resources and our strength." He sat down.

Brae looked down at his feet, all this felt so wrong.

Greyla spoke up next, addressing Odhar. "Did you know your daughters are missing?" She paused, eyeing Odhar up and down, her hand shaking as she gripped the top of her staff.

The colour drained out of Odhar's face.

He returned her questioning look with a blank stare and moved his gaze across to where Eyolas, his woman, sat.

Eyolas, tears now falling down her face, stood up and spilled her story to them all. About her daughters, about her attacker, about the note they left on the deer hide. And she told the other detail that came back to her....

135

"I remembered something else after the attack," Eyolas said shakily, "What the beast that attacked me was wearing around his middle."

Greyla interrupted, "If there *was* a beast...."

Eyolas scowled at her, "As he got up and stood over me there was something swinging from a kind of belt. It didn't register before. I think fear had blocked it out. Then it came back to me. He was wearing a belt of unicorn horns! And he was out in the woods when Marl was murdered! Stabbed by a unicorn horn!" Murmurs rose and spread around the room, rising, getting louder and louder.

As the rest of the room continued with their council, Odhar took Eyolas' arm and they left the hall.

Olga smoothed down Dark Fire's sleek coat along his back. His golden folded wings hung low and limp, he shook his mane and lowered his head, turning and bringing it round to gently nuzzle Olga's head. She laughed as his warm muzzle tickled her. Penna, Spit Fire and Heather stood, grateful for the opportunity to rest. Penna opened her blue-grey wings, still small and not fully grown, she practised flapping them up and down. Heather took out the water and took a sip, she offered it to Spit Fire. But Spit Fire suddenly turned his head away to his left. Ears pricked, his eyes widened, the whites showing. Then she heard it too. A slow, shuffling noise, like something large moving quietly, nearer, slowly, nearer. Beyond their torches the night was thick with blackness, there was no moon. Dark Fire moved beside Spit Fire, and beckoned silently for Penna to stand in front of the girls. The torches burned on, propped up against the rock. The slow shuffling came closer.

And then the Beast of Dekserot loomed into the torchlight, the orange light flickering on his face, glinting in his eye. He

136

snarled, a long drawn out snarl, tired and with one eye drooping, he surveyed the small plateau, the dark figures in the shadows not quite hidden enough and smelling strongly of fear.

Dark Fire stepped forward and opened his wings to their full span.

"Give up. Stop. Leave us. Your master is dead, we mean you no harm. Leave us now and we will not pursue you," he neighed.

The beast looked long and hard at Dark Fire, he roared loud and penetrating. He moved his head slowly, looking from side to side and then behind him.

Heather and Olga gasped, was he going to leave?

Dekserot turned back to face them and smelled the air, his nostrils flared and glowed red, smoke drifting up out of one.

And he took another step forward.

Spit Fire stepped forward, "Go! Leave! You are beaten."

Dekserot sniffed again. He lowered his head, the spikes along his neck quivered, moving along the length of his neck then disappeared with the rest of his body as the dark night enveloped the rest of him. He lowered his chest, crouching and took two steps closer. Pressed against the rock they could move back no further. They could see blood dripping from a wound under one of his front legs.

And the Beast of Dekserot jumped.

Spit Fire reared.

The girls screamed.

Penna neighed.

Dekserot opened his jaws, let out a mass of flames cascading over the plateau floor, the girls screamed and he swung his large head round to grab at Dark Fire. Dark Fire bent his head forward, concentrating the power through his horn and stopped the flames just short of the frightened group.

137

Spit Fire jumped to the side and struck the beast from behind as he writhed across the rock, knocking the torches flying, dislodging the contents and extinguishing the flames.

The beast's tails flicked back and slashed Spit Fire hard on his back legs, swiping him off his feet and knocking him to the ground. He lay there for a moment.

It was pitch black. The night surrounded them. Sounds became intensified, the rasping of the beast's breath, the scratching of his claws on the rocks, the scuffing of his scaly tails as he swished them across the plateau. The sound of Heather's heart beating in her chest.

Spit Fire got to his feet.

Dark fire reared and struck out, spitting sparks from his horn. Then received a sharp blow to his shoulder from the beast as he struck back.

Heather and Olga cried, they could just make out dim shapes in the shadows, occasionally highlighted by Dark Fire's horn or the glow from Dekserot's nostrils; a movement, a glint of teeth, a flash of a large yellow eye.

"I'm sure he'll be alright," neighed Penna, forgetting they couldn't understand her.

The blow brought on a greater rage inside Dark Fire, he charged blindly at the beast, screaming at him. Fighting ferociously, kicking and flying at him, till the beast backed off into the black. Dark Fire collapsed. His wings spread out before him. Heather and Olga ran up to him and dripped water onto his throbbing shoulder.

"It's... alright, I'm not too hurt," he panted. "Spit Fire, watch he, if he... comes back."

"Yes, anything, yes," Spit Fire whinnied a desperate reply.

Dekserot roared from behind the rocks nearby. Dark Fire closed his eyes, the pain was great. His old wound had opened

138

up and was bleeding badly. He tried to concentrate his remaining energy to his horn, *'Fire, we need fire,'* he thought. But he had no energy to create it.

They heard the beast coming back. Snarling and spitting he raised up to his full height, arched his neck back and spluttered a roar, belching a skirt of fire to attack the unicorns. Spit Fire jumped the flames as he reared and kicked, hooves slid off his scales, he swung his arched neck round to pierce Dekserot's armoured coat with his horn but missed as his two large tails came crashing his way. Spit Fire was hit again, but did not fall. Dark Fire raised himself up and fought again. It was a clash of claws, horns, manes and teeth, wings, tails and huge glaring eyes, a confusion of shapes in the darkness. The unicorns were tiring. Both were hurt, cut and bruised.

Spit Fire attacking from behind, broke through scales with his crashing hooves, the beast whipped his tails swiping round and whacked his attacker away. Knocked to his side, falling near the edge of the precipice Spit Fire lay. Heather scrambled over to him, cradling his head in her arms and kissing his muzzle.

Dekserot was getting weaker and weaker. He had lost scales and had received gashes from Spit Fires hooves, the wound from the Messenger's horn was deep and continued to bleed. He needed to rest. He couldn't breathe anymore fire. He started to back off away from the plateau, glancing back along the ledge to the edge where the rocks fell away vertically down the mountain side. In that moment, when he turned his head, Dark Fire, although weak and tired, reared with his wings spread wide, sprung forward, stretched out his neck and dug his horn deep, deep between the beast's scales, deep into the beast's heart.

Dekserot screamed a rasping roar, flinging his long neck

back round in a last desperate act of defence, craning his head towards Dark Fire, reaching, jaws open, teeth ripping, tearing at a wing, closing round his neck, a last desperate attempt to rid himself of his fatal attacker. They both fell. Crashing down to the rocky floor....

There was a terrible noise. Bangs and shaking sounds and terrible rumblings echoing around the mountains. Then all went silent.

The Beast of Dekserot was DEAD.

Olga and Heather cried out. They rushed over to the mound of shapes shrouded in darkness.

"Dark Fire!" they cried. They couldn't hear him breathing.

Penna rushed over and Spit Fire shakily got up from where he lay.

They tugged at the beast and its head rolled to the side, releasing its grip on Dark Fire's neck. Dark Fire took a deep breath in and shook his mane and head, snorting.

"My friend, you have saved us all!" whinnied Penna.

Dark Fire moved his majestic head. "I am broken."

The darkness was broken.

The night began to clear and a star shone brightly down at them. Olga bathed Dark Fire's head and wounds with water, and passed the water-skin to Heather, for Spit Fire.

Heather looked at Olga through the shadows, her face illuminated by the growing starlight, they were so exhausted. She lay her head on Spit Fire's back and Olga on Penna's and there they lay, where they had fallen, until the sun warmed their faces.

XIV

THE KING

In the morning light they looked around them. The dead beast lay across the plateau. A grim scene. Dark Fire, lay near to him, his legs to one side, his wings folded, his head bowed. Spit Fire and Penna stood to his side and the girls too. They held their breath as he lifted his head.

"We must go back to the herd, I can not fight again. Though I fear we are too late," Dark Fire spoke. "We will take the herd far away."

"No, no, we must try, we can not give up," Heather said anxiously, and walked over to the beast and picked up one of his large scales that had been ripped off in the fight. "Look, I will bring this, and we have Thoemanny's horns and Bas-Taibhse' claw. We will show the tribe, they will believe us."

Dark Fire placed his strength on one leg held out in front of him. With his back legs tucked underneath him he pushed himself up. He ached all over, his hindquarters throbbed from his earlier wound, and his bruised shoulder made him limp. He shook his long mane, blew dust through his nostrils, and took a few steps. Olga was at his side, she threw her arms around him and hugged him. They gathered their things.

Dark Fire and Spit Fire turned round to look at the fallen beast, the two stallions stood in silence, death deserved quiet, even the death of a terrible beast. And they turned to carefully walk down the mountains to the valley.

The Messenger stood over the King. She had stood there all night, guarding his soul. Tears fell down her face. He clung onto life. But lay fallen, pitiful. The whole herd stood around them, mourning their dying King.

Half way down the mountains the unicorns, girls, and Penna stopped briefly at a stream to rest and eat. Here the girls washed and re-bound Dark Fire's wound with the clay and herb mixture they had gathered on the island. Heather collected more young oak leaves and elfwort, that she found down the wooded slopes, crushing them in her hands and using them to rub over the unicorns' battered flanks. They ate the last of their hazelnut breads, and the unicorns and Penna grazed on the young shoots growing near the stream. Then, with replenished energy, they hurried on down to the valley.

After Odhar and Eyolas left the hall, Greyla took the unicorn horn from around the Chief's neck.

"We will call upon the gods!" she cried out, and was met by a rising applause of beating sticks and fists. The women gathered around her, bringing her the crushed herbs and salts to heat in the horn. The Chief still slouched at the back. Two men carried him to the circle. A young girl passed the carved bone bowl and they offered him strong barley whisky. He drank. The drums beat out a rising crescendo.

Greyla took the horn, lit its contents and inhaled. Her old bent frame shook then jerked upright, standing straight and tall. She lifted up her arms to the fire now burning high in the centre of the hall.

"Taiu, god of fire! Oh most powerful one! Come down to us! Destroy the unicorns and their dragon!"

"No!" shouted Brae across the room to the shocked faces, "the unicorns should not be destroyed!"

The crowd rose up, "What are you saying?"

Two watchers grabbed his arms and wrestled him to the side speaking into his face, "We need their horns! Be quiet!"

"Horns are useless without the unicorn," Brae muttered bitterly, struggling in their grip.

Greyla glowered and picked up her chant, "Cleanse us of evil within our tribes! ...We give ourselves to you!" She shook, cackling, head thrown back, only the whites of her eyes showing, jolting nearer and nearer to the flames till she was almost upon them, her body prone, a silhouette. Some of the other women took the horn, breathed in its incantation and joined her dance to the flames.

The horn was passed to the Chief. He breathed in long and deeply.

"What do you see? What do you see?" cried the gathered crowd.

The Chief unsteadily got up and half walked half staggered to the fire. He upturned the horn and shook its contents into the flames, they crackled and sparked, blue and green.

With his hand still held high above the fire he shouted, "Come on! Do your worst! Oh mighty Taiu!" He paused. The flames began to grow, and in their depths he saw a dark black winged unicorn rising up, with three more unicorns beside him and two small figures, like girls, holding hands. Then the vision had gone.

"I see... I see *nothing!*" He cast down the horn and stumbled back to the furs he'd been resting on.

The crowd hushed.

The trees thinned and the land opened out onto the grand majestic valley. It should have been a beautiful sight, but there was an unnatural stillness and silence hanging in the air. Rain clouds hung heavy at the far end of the valley, great cumulonimbus towering up into the sky. Dark Fire and Spit Fire looked at each other, they both could sense something bad had happened. Despite their injuries they rushed on with hopeless urgency.

They reached the herd.

They were too late.

The girls ran ahead seeing the fallen King. A long spear stuck upright, out of his chest, a forlorn band of feathers and blue, fluttered from it, attached below the spearhead. The mark of the Trosban. They cried out in shocked horror. They fell at his paralysed prostrate frame, ashamed of being 'man' and sobbed.

"My children," softly nickered the Messenger. "You are not to blame." Another tear fell from her face. "Will you ease his pain? You two can remove this weapon of man-thing."

They looked up at her, standing massive and brilliant and sorrowful, golden outlined against the dark rain clouds.

They stood up and grasped the spear between them and slowly pulled it out, casting it to the ground.

The King gasped and opened his eyes. "Thank you. Now...."

he spluttered, "you two are brave and courageous. And wise beyond your years. Use your wisdom... and go.... Go change the *world*." He closed his eyes. Heather was sat near to his face, Olga knelt down and stroked his ears. "And bring *peace*." And he breathed out, his last.

The massing dark clouds closed in, like a cloak of night and the rain fell.

A faint shimmer of light, highlighted by the falling rain, lifted from the King's body rising upwards, his soul. Olga and Heather watched his spirit rise up to the heavens, and as they looked, the clouds broke apart and they could see way up into an opening of blue, and there, appeared a new bright star. It was like the legends of old told. Like the paintings on the cave walls at the Sacre Ogof. Now they understood fully what they meant.

The girls went down to the stream and brought out rocks to place around the King. They picked flowers and laid them on his mane. They knelt down in quiet, then left with the rest of the herd to the higher grazing up the valley.

Dark Fire, Spit Fire, the Messenger, Penna, the elders: Samant, Solas and Saor, all gathered round Heather and Olga. The girls brought their deerskin bags and took out Bas-Taibhse's claw, Thoemanny's horned headdress and Dekserot's scale, the remains of the three beasts. And placed them down on the damp earth in the centre of the gathered council.

"The beasts are no more," neighed Dark Fire solemnly. "Yet, man-things killed your King. And they remain a powerful threat." He shook his mane.

The Messenger spoke. "Dark Fire. You have saved us from these three beasts. You are the son of the old King. By right you are now our King." And she bowed almost down to the ground. The unicorns and Penna all bowed, the girls lowered their heads and went down on one knee.

Dark Fire bowed his head. "Messenger, elders, Penna, I could not have succeeded without the help of Spit Fire, Heather and Olga, who have risked their lives to protect me." He pawed the ground. "We will go to meet with the man-things. We will show them what is left of the beasts, and Heather and Olga will tell them our story. But tonight, we rest."

As evening drew in and the watery sun sank below the horizon, the girls lit a fire to warm them through the night. Penna had curled up next to them, and Dark Fire and Spit Fire stood near in the warmth of the flames.

Heather awoke in the night. The starlight was so bright. A bright star shone in the sky. It grew larger, a flash with a sparkling tail, shooting across the sky, ripping through the darkness, downwards, heading across the valley and beyond. She woke Olga, and Penna, who had been resting her head on Olga's lap, they looked up and followed the star's path. It disappeared into the distance. A second later there was a loud bang. A second after, a ripple went through the ground like an earthly wave and the mountains behind them shook sending rocks crashing below. A faint orange glow bled into the horizon where it had disappeared.

"It is a sign," neighed Penna, "a ball of fire."

"What does she say?" asked Heather, but Olga was non the wiser.

"A fireball," neighed Dark Fire, who had been watching half asleep.

Heather looked over to Olga, a little anxiously. "That's towards our lands."

The sky lit up for a second time, but this time it was the dawn.

Heather and Olga, carrying the three beasts remains, the Messenger, Dark Fire, Spit Fire and Penna began their journey to the tribe's village. Olga rode on the Messenger as Dark Fire was not able to carry her, she carried the spear that had killed the King. Heather rode on Spit Fire. They walked and trotted, a steady pace, collecting their thoughts, unsure of how they would be received.

They crossed the streams and hills that led to the deer woods, their village lands, their village.... As their hill came into view, they noticed smoke trailing away from one side of it. Heather and Olga's hearts leapt to their throats. Their village, their parents? Smoke like this meant fire.

Panicking they cantered fast through the woodlands until they came to a large crater eaten out of the side of their hill. The red sandstone and igneous rock exposed, jagged, trees around had been scorched and burnt, the crater centre still burning and smoking. They rushed on up towards the watchers' caves, they still stood. Heather and Olga dismounted and rushed inside their home.

Inside it was cold and empty, a few things had fallen down, it was abandoned, deserted. A thin layer of ash lay on everything. They ran out and beckoned to the unicorns to follow them on up to the rest of their village on the hilltop.

They came to the ramparts. The poles still stood upright but the gates swung open. They looked in, aghast. Half the village was destroyed. Huts burnt to the ground and still burning. Wood hens ran about squawking, Olga caught one and picked it up to comfort it. The place was deserted.

The great hall was still standing, and as they walked across the clearing they heard movement from within. They called out to their mother and father. Feet shuffled and moving into the doorway, they could make out a bent figure....

It looked like Greyla, the elder. They had grown to dislike her in recent times as she had chosen a disliking to them. The figure bent over a staff. The girls moved slowly nearer, followed by the unicorns and Penna. The figure leaning heavily on the staff, stepped out into the light. It was the Chief.

He raised his head and looked on in disbelief at the two girls standing in front of him, with three powerful unicorns and a small winged horse standing behind them, like his vision in the flames. The girl Olga, stood holding his own spear he had left pierced in the flesh of a large grey winged unicorn. And the golden unicorn he recognised as the one who had kicked him in the head. He stared.

Olga spoke, fighting back the tears. "What's happened? Where are our mother and father? Where is everyone?"

Stunned and ignoring the fact that there were three unicorns standing in his village, the Chief replied. "A ball of fire. Fell from the sky. Half the village destroyed." He sank his head in his hand, still supporting himself on his staff with the other. After rubbing his face he looked again at the scene standing before him. "Unicorns?"

"Yes. Our mother and father?" Olga returned, anxious to know if they were alright.

"Odhar's lass. Your mother and father left for the sun temple with the others. After the fire hit, all ran for their lives. Only I remained." Then, raising his voice. "Why have you brought the one that tried to *kill* me *here*?"

"Chief." Olga bowed her head in respect. "Unicorns have saved us. These unicorns have saved us. They fought the three great beasts that have attacked our tribes and the beasts are now dead!" She shook as she spoke, clenching her fist tight around the Chief's spear. "Unicorns must not be hunted! They mean us no harm unless they are attacked." She swallowed back her tears, and said with venom. "You killed their King!"

Heather took her arm and brought her close to her, shushing her. Then stood up tall and addressed the Chief.

"You must listen to us. There can be no more blood shed." Heather took out the Beast of Thoemanny's horned headdress and his belt of unicorn horns. "This beast was a man like us. Only, a giant man." She grabbed Olga's bag and tipped out the large scale belonging to Dekserot and Bas-Taibhse's claw. "And here is the scale off the beast that attacked you in the mountains. And another beast's claw."

The Chief just stared. He sat down on a rock beside the doorway and sank his head in his hands.

"Come on Olga," said Heather and bundled the stuff back into their bags and mounted the unicorns. They rode past the Chief, who glanced up, awestruck to see the girls sitting gracefully, riding the unicorns through the village, and on down the far side of the hill heading for Solas Aor, the sun temple.

Cantering down the gentle slopes and over a hill they could see a crowd gathered at the temple. They slowed down to a trot.

Greyla, standing in the centre, performing another ritual, saw them first. She exclaimed and shrieked. The whole crowd turned. They saw four dark shapes approaching, silhouetted by the drifts of smoke and the burning village. One black shape in the middle outstretched its wings, flapping them antagonistically. As they came nearer their shapes took form and they could clearly see they were unicorns. And riding on top of two of them were two figures. She strained her eyes and they came closer. The mounted figures, she knew their faces, they were the wayward girls, the two sisters that stole their horses, Odhar's children! Greyla cursed, her fists clenched at the sky. The crowd shrank back.

Eyolas broke through the throngs of people. She ran, tears streaming down her face, fearless of the unicorns. Grateful to see her girls again, well and strong. Olga and Heather jumped down from their rides. Tired and tearful they threw their arms round their mother who didn't stop hugging them and kissing them. Odhar stood at a short distance, away from the crowd. They ran on to greet him.

Eyolas stayed beside the unicorns. She reached up her hand to the Messenger and stroked her neck. She turned to Dark Fire, observing his wounds, and offered her hand to his muzzle. He bent his handsome head down to touch her face and she closed her eyes and kissed his muzzle.

She whispered, "Thank you for returning my daughters safely. I prayed you would. Thank you." She spoke to them all, stroking Spit Fire's pale golden mane and Penna's blueish feathery crest.

Heather and Olga stepped back. They emptied the contents of their bags before the watching crowd. "We took these from the beasts! *THE THREE BEASTS*! Which have attacked you. It was *never* the unicorns! They are our friends. They saved us and you." Heather shouted to the people.

Brae put up his fist to the sky, shouting in agreement.

Olga held up high the horned headdress of Thoemanny's and his belt of unicorn horns. "And this belonged to a man! A giant man! Masquerading as a beast!"

Eyolas gasped and put both hands up to her face.

Olga continued, "He had trained the other two beasts. Trained them to kill! They are now dead. They are all dead."

Greyla started a low wailing.

"There must be no more bloodshed," Dark Fire neighed. "I am the King of all unicorns and winged horses. There must be

150

peace."

Greyla shut up. She had heard Dark Fire speaking clearly.

The Chief came walking up slowly behind the group of unicorns. He put his hand out to the Messenger.

The Messenger stared back at the man-thing. She could smell him. He was the man-thing that killed their King. She looked at him with hatred, her eyes showing their white as he got down on both his knees. She could easily kill him now. But he stayed there and lowered his head, spreading his arms out in front of him.

"He is asking forgiveness," whinnied Dark Fire.

The Messenger stood motionless. She snorted, then reared up tall to her full height. And then brought her hooves crashing down on the earth next to the Chief. He flinched. He looked up slowly, the sweat pouring off his face and got up.

"I have thought," the Chief paused. "They are right! And we have been misled!" He looked across at Greyla standing in the middle of the stones. "We have been *misled*!"

Greyla loosed her grip on the unicorn horn and let it drop from her hand. Her bent frame, swayed against her stick, seemed smaller. She walked, bent, away from the stone circle and left the group. The crowd, led by Brae, cautiously began to walk towards the unicorns.

Heather and Olga remembered the King's dying words: *"Use your wisdom, oh you, wiser beyond your years, to change the world and bring peace."*

XV

THE LIVING STONE

*H*eather ran down the hill through the bright orange and yellows of the autumn trees. Sun dappling her face. Laughing, sheer delight, freedom, peace. The tribe had re-built their village. The surrounding tribes: the Tarbraes, Arthruads, Iolaires and Cabhairs had all helped. They had mourned the ones they'd lost and built a new Henge to remember them by. And they respected the unicorns. They lived in peace.

Dark Fire and Spit Fire had visited the girls at the end of the summer and took them to the valley to see a surprise; two new additions to the herd. The Messenger had another foal, a filly, named Siochain, meaning peace in the old language, she had the gift, she was a Messenger. And Penna had a foal too, a filly named Saoirse, freedom.

Heather picked up a handful of autumn leaves and threw them at Olga. She ducked and picked up a handful to throw back. Heather tossed her hair to one side, screwing her face up to miss them, and scooped up another large handful in her arms and threw them back.

"Ow!" said Olga, "There was a stone in that!" She reached down and picked up the offending rock. Turning it over in her palm and observing its crystalline colours.

"Look, it's a crystal!" she exclaimed.

Then Heather came over and marvelled at the unusual stone. "No, it's an amber, no, a ruby."

"No! A turquoise! Sapphire... and violet, like the flowers, an amethyst!" disputed Olga.

"No, it's none of those," said Heather. "It's the living stone! The one that took us into the sea-caves! But I threw it away into the sea in the cave?"

"Yes, it is... it's heavy and warm, and the colours are changing. But how can it be the one from the sea caves? It must be another one," reasoned Olga. "Look! ...And it has an eye!"

"Throw it away!" said Heather. "Before you can't!" And she took it from Olga's hand and ran on down the bank, Olga running after her, and she threw it into the stream as the water tumbled away from the waterfall....

Author's note on Prehistoric Britain.

I have always had a fascination with our prehistoric past and believe prehistoric societies lived highly complex, intricate and intelligent lives.

Stone Age people survived. In a land of cave-lions, bears, hyenas, and rhinoceros, they survived, when all they had was fire and stone and will.

This work is pure fiction, but I like to speculate on what could have been possible, considering current archeological evidence:

Until roughly 8,000 years ago Britain was once joined to Europe by Doggerland, a submerged land mass, which would have enabled travel and knowledge across Europe. Although the oldest standing stones in Britain date from 3000BC in Orkney, there is new evidence of megalithic structures in North Western France from 5000BC and older structures from 9000BC in Gobekli Tepe in Turkey. Could it be that some older stone circles existed but have been lost to time? Or that ancient megalithic sites were built on earlier sites? The earliest evidence of textile use comes from wild flax fibres being spun, dyed and knotted, dating back to 30,000 years ago from Dzudzuana Cave, Georgia. Though there's no evidence from Britain, could cloth have been woven and worn here in the Mesolithic?

To survive, prehistoric people must have had a strong connection and respect for the earth. Despite our advancement and technologies, many species are threatened with extinction today, yet each species is vital to life on earth, and to our own survival.

Unicorns have lived in numerous fables of many eastern and western civilizations throughout history. Solid evidence of their existence has yet to be found, but their elusiveness, power and magic lives on in our imaginations.

ABOUT THE AUTHOR

Sally E K Warner is an artist and designer, with a BA in Furniture Design and an MSc in Architecture: Advanced Environmental and Energy Studies.

Sally wrote The III Beasts & The Unicorns when she was 7. Reading it later in life to her own children, she decided to re-write it, publish it and make it into a film.

Follow your dreams.

www.sallyek.co.uk
Instagram: Redhairanddangerous

Printed in Poland
by Amazon Fulfillment
Poland Sp. z o.o., Wrocław